I0679133

The Hidden Enquiries of Sherlock Holmes

Arthur Hall

Edited by David Marcum

Paperback ISBN 978-1-80424-616-0
ePub ISBN 978-1-80424-617-7
PDF ISBN 978-1-80424-618-4

MX Publishing
335 Princess Park Manor, Royal Drive,
London, N11 3GX
www.mxpublishing.com

Cover design by Awan

Arthur Hall was born in Aston, Birmingham, UK, in 1944. His interest in writing began during his schooldays and served as a growing ambition to become an author.

Years later, his first novel 'Sole Contact' was an espionage story about an ultra-secret government department known as 'Sector Three' and has been followed, to date, by five sequels.

Other works include seven 'rediscovered' cases from the files of Sherlock Holmes, three collections of short stories featuring The Great Detective, two collections of bizarre tales and two novels about an adventurer called 'Bernard Kramer', as well as several contributions to the ongoing anthology, 'The MX Book of New Sherlock Holmes Stories'.

His only ambition, apart from being published more widely, is to attend the premier of a film based on one of his novels, ideally at The Odeon, Leicester Square.

He lives in the West Midlands, United Kingdom, where he often walks other people's dogs as he attempts to formulate new plots.

His work can be seen at: arthurhallsbooksite.blogspot.com, and the author can be contacted at: arthurhall7777@aol.co.uk

By the same author:

Contents:

The Adventure of the African Prospector

From a reference in 'The Blanched Soldier'.

I looked at my friend, Mr Sherlock Holmes the consulting detective, curiously. He did not lift his eyes from the morning edition of *The Standard,* but adjusted his position in his armchair while blowing out a cloud of fragrant smoke. That did not prevent him from noticing my interest, however.

"I take it that it is my new pipe that has attracted your attention, Watson?"

"I was certain that I had not seen it before now."

He looked up slowly, and from the other side of the empty fireplace I could see a glint in his eyes, or it could have been a reflection of the early summer sunlight.

"I received it in the first post, before you presented yourself for breakfast. It is a gift from someone who was of great assistance to me during my time in Montague Street. You may have seen mention of Sir James Saunders in the dailies from time to time."

"The famous dermatologist? I recall that he had some success with identifying that outbreak in the northern counties, several years ago. But why would he have sent you a gift? Has the pipe some special significance?"

Holmes smiled. "No, old fellow, only that I once mentioned to him that I have a small collection. It was the accompanying letter that was of interest."

"He requires your services, then?"

"Precisely, and I shall be glad to aid him in any way that I can, to discharge the debt that I owe him. It is a case of double-murder that he mentions." He extracted his pocket-watch from his waistcoat and looked at it briefly. "I am to catch the mid-morning train for Gorhampton Priors within the hour. Pray pack an overnight bag, if you would care to accompany me."

Having complied with this, I stood next to my friend on a rather crowded platform in Fenchurch Street Station within the hour. While in the hansom that had conveyed us from our lodgings I had noted that, as often on such occasions, he had brought no visible baggage. His requirements, he stated on more than one occasion previously, were no more than a clean collar and a toothbrush.

Our wait was short. Holmes had no sooner purchased our tickets than the train came to rest before us with a squeal of brakes and surrounded by wreathes of smoke. We were fortunate in finding a compartment to ourselves in the first smoker we approached, and I contained my curiosity with difficulty until the outskirts of the capital were left behind.

"I think, Holmes, that there is time for you to tell me something of what we are about to undertake, before we reach our destination," I said then.

He settled himself in the seat opposite mine and produced his pipe, which he lit. I refrained from doing likewise, as I was more interested in discovering the nature of the task before us.

"The letter from Sir James was quite extensive," he began as smoke swirled above him. "You may have wondered, Watson, why I did not show it to you. The reason is that I was uncertain of your participation after your recent bout of influenza, which I know taxed your strength severely."

I have never doubted my friend's concern, but I could not help wondering whether the nature of Sir James' assistance, years ago, was a secondary reason why the letter had been withheld from me. Holmes had been unusually vague, as to the specifics of it.

"Pray do not concern yourself. I am fully recovered."

"Excellent! My work would be of lesser satisfaction to me, without my Boswell."

"Holmes," I said as the train rattled over the points and took a new direction. "What is it that has caused Sir James to consult you?"

"Two of his guests have been murdered. The local force is mystified, and have concluded that the perpetrator is a vagabond who has been seen in the surrounding villages. They have therefore concentrated their enquiries in that direction and Sir James has indicated that he is grateful for that since he views the official detective, Inspector Winster Soames who I have never made the acquaintance of, as an incompetent idiot. It was after forming this opinion that he recalled my profession."

"Were the visitors killed at the same time?" I asked, after considering for a moment.

"The murders occurred on the same afternoon, at a garden party held by Sir James."

"When was this?"

"Three days past."

"How were they committed?"

"It was arsenic poisoning, according to the police pathologist, administered in the wine that was served."

"Did Sir James mention any additional features, or anything of peculiar significance?"

"He did indeed, and it is the reason why he could not confide completely with Inspector Soames."

I raised my eyebrows. "What was it, then?"

"The element that attracted me at once. You see, Watson, Sir James is an excellent fellow, but he has always been possessed of a strong fear of becoming the subject of ridicule. When an event such as this occurs at his home it is disturbing enough, but when the perpetrator appears to be a younger brother who has long been thought dead, the resulting scandal to the family seems to him unendurable."

"Did he actually see the murderer?"

"It appears that one of the victims saw a man looking down from a window. She spoke his name and pointed as she expired."

"Was he seen by any of the others present?"

"Apparently only Sir James. Everyone else saw only a blank window."

"Possibly it was a reflection or an illusion. It is known that this happens to death-bed cases occasionally before they pass from this life, although that does not explain what Sir James saw. At any rate, Holmes, this cannot be the truth of it. How often have you proved that so-called supernatural incidents are nothing but trickery?"

"Quite so, old fellow, and I fully expect the result of this investigation to be similar. However, I see from my pocket-watch that we have scarcely ten minutes left before we arrive at Gorhampton Priors Station, so I suggest that we continue this discussion later."

He had made no mention of it, but Holmes must have telegraphed Sir James to indicate the time of our arrival, since a shining landau awaited us. The driver, who apparently had long been in service there, lost no time in cheerfully conveying us through a succession of leafy lanes until we came upon the open fields that surrounded Darkly Grange, Sir James' ancestral home.

We soon found ourselves upon a wide gravel path, with tall bushes on either side. Someone with extensive knowledge of the art of topiary had shaped them expertly into various animal species.

The house was not at all as I had imagined. Holmes had mentioned that it dated from the time of the Tudors, but it was not typical of that style. Both wings appeared to have succumbed to the ravages of time and been removed, with obvious repairs to the main structure. What remained was a building of three storeys, the upper two boasting fifteen windows each and the ground floor bisected by an arch that was the entrance to the courtyard.

The driver brought the landau to a halt and we alighted. Before it had disappeared beneath the arch the massive iron-studded door swung open and a middle-aged man of average height descended the steps, obviously pleased to see us.

"Mr Holmes," he shook my friend's hand vigorously, "how good of you to come."

"I am very glad to make your acquaintance once more, Sir James." Holmes disengaged himself and gestured in my direction. "Allow me to introduce my friend and colleague, Doctor John Watson."

Our host seemed equally glad of my presence, and quickly ushered us into the house. It was like many I had seen before, with oak-panelled walls surmounted by ancestral portraits and crossed swords. Suits of polished armour stood sentry-like in corners and niches. After being shown to our rooms by a butler who seemed unfamiliar with the configuration of the place, we joined Sir James for luncheon.

Our host proved to serve an excellent table, and chatted enthusiastically throughout the meal. I could sense that Holmes was growing tired of this prevarication and had, as was usual for him, consumed little.

"I understand, Sir James," he said as our host paused to drink, "that you are experiencing some difficulty, the precise details of which you have not yet informed me. If you would care to elaborate, Watson and myself will be pleased to render what assistance we can."

Sir James replaced his glass, suddenly more serious. "I have indeed found these last few days most trying, as has everyone here. Indeed, I can remember no time to compare."

"Your letter mentioned the murders of two of your guests."

"That was three days ago, at Lady Anne's garden party. I still call it that, though my good lady passed on five years past. Mrs Margaret Feldeane, a widowed lady from the village, and her son, barely eighteen, keeled over and died near that bush you see there." He gestured through the high window, across the lawn to a topiary shape of a hen. "Poor young fellow, about to enter the army too. Would have made a great name for himself, I'm sure."

"It was arsenic poisoning, according to the police pathologist?"

"That was his conclusion. Fortunately, if I may put it so, only Mrs Feldeane and her son drank from the bottle. The wine was an Alsace vintage, known to be a favourite of hers and ordered specially. It was a startling and sad affair, but the strangest thing occurred after the poor lady collapsed." He shook his head, incredulously. "You gentlemen cannot know it, but I had a younger brother, Gilbert, who was at one time engaged to Mrs Feldeane before he embarked upon an expedition to prospect for gold in Africa. Apparently she forced him to choose between her and the voyage and he chose, unwisely in my opinion, to depart. That was years ago, and he has long since been lost and given up for dead.

The relevance is that she looked up at the house as she died, and cried out, 'Oh, it is you, Gilbert!' as she expired."

"It is not unusual, Sir James," I said then, "for the dying to experience visions of those they have known. I do not think we should place too much credence on the incident."

He appeared no less perplexed, and hesitated before continuing. "I could accept that Doctor, indeed I heard as much from Inspector Soames, fool that he is. But I was with Mrs Feldeane and immediately turned to where she stared in her last moments." He hesitated again. "It seems that I saw what no one else except she had noticed. For an instant I perceived but faintly, the face of my brother grimly observing us. Then it was gone."

Holmes nodded slowly. "Did this – apparition, shall we call it? - appear to say anything, to gesticulate or move?"

"Not at all. It had vanished before I had realised what I was seeing."

"Do you recall the window where it appeared?"

"Later, when some of the shock had passed, I returned to the garden and looked again at the back of the house. I would swear that the window where I had seen the vision is the ninth from the left side, on the second floor. Together with the groom and my new butler, Melhuish, I examined every room on both the first and second stories. Most of that part of the house lies unused, has done for a considerable time, but I can assure you that we discovered nothing out of the ordinary."

"Has anything else of an unusual nature occurred in your household, Sir James?" Holmes asked after a moment. "Pray be precise as to details, however insignificant they may seem."

Sir James pushed away his empty plate. "Now that you mention it, Mr Holmes, I suppose you could say that there has been rather a lot of activity at Darkly Grange recently. Usually, you know, we live quiet lives here, but I suppose everyone has their ups and downs."

"Kindly elaborate," my friend requested with a trace of impatience.

"Well, let me see. About two months ago I acquired a magnificent Cezanne. It is a self-portrait of the artist, but quite different from the famous one, as it shows him as a younger man. I have always collected art, and I consider this my crowning achievement. My cousin, Mr Erasmus Bartley was rather jealous, but that was not unexpected. He is a collector also, somewhat more fanatically so than myself. When I invited him to view the picture he offered to buy it, but it is not for sale."

"I would be delighted to see it," Holmes said surprisingly.

"Of course." Our host continued, "Shortly afterwards, Rowens died suddenly. He was my butler for many years, and our local doctor thought it was his heart since it had troubled him previously. I had another visit from Erasmus about then, to repeat his offer. He lives not far away, a couple of miles over the hill at Mortley Manor, and this time he did me a bit of good. Poor Rowens was not yet cold, if you will forgive me for putting it like that, before Courtney replaced him at my cousin's recommendation. It saved me the trouble of consulting an agency, references and all that. I was grateful to Erasmus at the time, but I'm not so sure now."

"Courtney proved unsatisfactory?" I presumed.

"Not in his work. The fact is, he left Darkly Grange just before the garden party. I recall that it was the night after Mrs Feldeane and her son arrived. I intended them to stay for a day or two." He spread his hands in an incredulous gesture. "The fellow just let himself out and went in the early hours!"

"Curious," Holmes commented as the dessert arrived.

"I thought perhaps he had received word of a dying relative or something of the sort, but he could at least have informed me."

"One would have expected so," said I.

There was silence between us while we ate, my friend sparingly, until Sir James put down his spoon in conclusion.

"That, I believe, is all I can tell you. Except that Melhuish was subsequently supplied to me by the agency that I should have used in the first place. Oh, and there was the kitchen maid Alice, who I had to dismiss."

Holmes leaned forward in his seat, his interest aroused further. "May I ask why?"

"I cannot tolerate dishonesty. Food and wine was missing from the kitchen four or five times. It wasn't as if I didn't pay the girl enough."

My friend said little more as we drank our coffee.

"Sir James," he began when our cups were empty. "There are clear indications that whoever is responsible for the deaths of Mrs

Feldeane and her son is familiar with both your house and your visitors. Otherwise how, for example, did he know which window would best enable his victims to see him, and how was he able to identify the wine which Mrs Feldeane preferred? There are also other indications. It would be as well, I think, if I examined the back of the house from the exact spot where you and she stood at the moment of her passing, but first I would appreciate it if you would describe the other guests."

"Since my wife passed, fewer of our former guests have attended. They are mostly my own friends now, such as Captain Tebbitt and his wife and Mr Jonathan Strider. Mrs Georgina Gough was also present, and Miss Crowther. Some of them brought friends with them who are unknown to me, as they have always been free to do. All of these reside either in the north of the country or, in the case of Mr Strider, in Plymouth. They usually stay for a night after the party and then return to their homes. I fear that the tradition will not be continued henceforth."

We adjourned then to the garden as Holmes had suggested. Sir James indicated the place near the topiary hen where he had stood when he glimpsed the face at the window, and from there my friend examined the rear of the building. I saw the faintest smile pass over his face, but then he shook his head and I knew he had reached no definite conclusion.

"Very well," he said then. "Perhaps, Sir James, you will now allow Watson and myself to see the Cezanne. I have always maintained an interest in art, at least since I was fortunate enough to see a Da Vinci when I travelled through Italy a few years ago."

"Of course!" Our host's face lit up at the mention of the subject that was so beloved to him. "Come this way, gentlemen."

He led us back into the house and along a corridor that ran the entire length of the building. Before we had progressed halfway he stopped before a sturdy door and produced a key. We entered a dark and spacious room.

Sir James lit an oil lamp near the door, and then another, and we saw that we were surrounded by portraits of unsmiling gentlemen in various styles of attire.

"Your ancestors, presumably?" Holmes asked.

"They are, though the exhibition is incomplete." Our host ushered us along the room until we were confronted by a large portrait that was unlike the others. "Here it is, my Cezanne. Magnificent, isn't it?"

Holmes scrutinized it for several minutes. "The brushwork is exquisite. The detail, both in the features and the background, is unmistakeably his work. Many a collector, and indeed public galleries, must envy you this, Sir James."

"Undoubtedly this is so, but while it remains in my possession it will not leave this room. I have considered leaving it to a museum upon my death, but for the moment the matter is undecided."

"A noble thought, indeed."

I, without Holmes' enthusiasm, examined the collection as we retraced our steps. I reflected that his knowledge of art was yet another side of my friend that I had been unaware of until now. Over the years I had learned something of many of the facets of his personality, but evidently he could still surprise me.

"Are any of these portraits in the likeness of your brother Gilbert?" he enquired of our host as we returned along the aisle.

Sir James shook his head. "As far as I am aware there is but one picture of him as an adult in existence, commissioned a few months before Gilbert undertook the African expedition by Erasmus. It is still part of his collection."

"Excellent! Would it be possible for us to accompany you on a visit to your cousin tomorrow? I have a mind to view his collection also."

Our host looked rather taken aback at this unexpected request, but readily agreed. "You will find him an interesting fellow, though rather boorish in some of his ways. Do you know, Mr Holmes, he ran away and joined a circus before he was seventeen years old. When he eventually returned to the family it was as a man who had experienced many adventures. What a life he must have had!"

I caught a glance that told me that my friend had formed a theory, but knew he would say nothing until he felt the time was right.

"I wonder from where his love of art developed."

"Perhaps it was inherited, as was mine. He used to tell us stories of his exploits. Once, when he had indulged in too many glasses of port, he related to Lady Anne and myself a saga of his involvement with a gang of art thieves in Paris during the circus's visit there, but of course we never took him seriously. I am quite sure that many of his stories were exaggerated."

We remained in that room for a considerable time, so that I became depressed by the closeness of its windowless walls. My two companions seemed unaffected, and the discussion continued with my occasional contributions. At last we emerged into the corridor, and Sir James consulted his pocket-watch remarking that, to his surprise, dinner would be served in little more than an hour.

"How time speeds by when you are absorbed," he observed.

"Will tomorrow afternoon be convenient for our visit to your cousin?" Holmes asked him then.

"Oh, there is no need to make an appointment. Erasmus turns up here whenever the mood takes him, so he can hardly complain if we do the same."

"Thank you, Sir James. I am confident that I will have some news for you afterwards." He ignored our host's look of pleasant surprise. "There is one more question I must ask you, if you would be so kind."

"I am at your service."

"It concerns Mrs Feldeane. Since you mentioned that your brother was once engaged to her, I presume that she once lived near here."

"That is so. She grew up near the village. It could have been that she and Gilbert married in our local church on his return from Africa but, as you know, it was not to be."

"And so, when he was declared dead she married another?"

He nodded. "After a respectable time had passed she wed Mr Andrew Feldeane, and moved to his family home in Northumberland."

"But during her early life, did she have a close friend or confidante?"

Sir James looked puzzled for a moment, then: "Yes, of course. Miss Janet Crenthorpe. She is unmarried, and still lives near the village."

"Then that is where me must go in the morning, if you will kindly furnish us with the address."

Dinner was an elaborate and, for me, very satisfying meal. Holmes, as was usual for him, ate only a small proportion. This, I observed, was not only because of his poor appetite, but also because of his responses to Sir James' enquiries regarding our past adventures. My friend was polite, as always, but guarded in his revelations. This continued further into the evening, when we smoked and drank brandy with Sir James in the library. Earlier than was our custom, we left our host in a jovial mood and retired.

We breakfasted alone, Melhuish having informed us that his master had risen early in order to supervise the repairs to stock fencing in the north pasture. He had not returned as we finished our meal and set off for Miss Crenthorpe's house.

The village was near the edge of the estate, but easily within walking distance. Sir James had furnished us with precise directions and we came upon a group of thatched cottages near the vicarage, as he had described. At the end of the long wall of the Reverend's garden stood a tiny house, white with black beams and a tall chimney. Holmes knocked lightly upon the door, which opened to reveal a woman of prim appearance with pince-nez perched on an aquiline nose.

"Good morning," he began cheerfully. "I hope you will forgive this intrusion. My name is Sherlock Holmes, I am a consulting detective and would be grateful for a few minutes of your time."

She gave us a worried look which softened quite suddenly.

"Why yes, I believe I have read of you."

"My companion," he indicated me, "Doctor John Watson, is fond of exaggerating my trifling successes in print."

"It is an honour to meet you sir, but what brings you to me? Have I unknowingly committed a crime?"

"Nothing of the sort," Holmes smiled. "We are making enquiries on behalf of Sir James Saunders, regarding the recent deaths at Darkly Grange. I believe you knew one of the victims, Mrs Margaret Feldeane, and it is she about whom we are seeking information."

The pince-nez glinted as she nodded her bird-like head.

"My poor friend. We were close when she was Margaret Derrow, it is true, but I have seen little of her since her marriage. However, come in gentlemen, and I will try to assist you."

We thanked her and entered into a narrow corridor leading to a spotless sitting-room. I saw at once that the furniture was perfectly positioned around the fireplace, and the tiny desk in the corner shone from much polishing. I concluded that, being unmarried, she poured her energies into maintaining an immaculate home, and possibly into service at the nearby church also.

When we were seated she offered refreshments, which we refused as we had not long eaten breakfast. She arranged herself upon a chair that faced us both with an expectant expression.

"Can you remember anything of Mrs Feldeane that could aid us in our investigation?" Holmes began. "For example, do you know of anyone who had reason to dislike her, or harbour hatred? I understand that this is an unusual request but, as you will appreciate, whoever is responsible for her death did not become so without reason."

Miss Crenthorpe spent a few moments in thoughtful concentration, before shaking her head slowly. "Throughout our childhood and after, I can recall but one occasion when Margaret was involved in a heated exchange. We had walked a long way into the countryside and realised quite late in the day that we would not be able to return before dark. Margaret, after some thought, led us through the forest on Lord Northingham's estate because that would shorten the distance by a few miles. We had the misfortune to meet the gamekeeper, Grimforth, always an unpleasant fellow, who was quite rude. Margaret told him what she thought of his attitude in no uncertain terms, and after the oaths he directed at us he troubled us no further. Apart from that incident, her disposition was always calm and placid, inviting no animosity from anyone."

"Was there anything about her behaviour that might have caused offence to her friends or neighbours, however accidentally?"

This time Miss Crenthorpe needed no time to consider.

"Nothing," she answered immediately, "and as she grew older that became less likely still."

"Why do you say that, Miss Crenthorpe?"

"Because of her health. She became prone to seizures, which would strike when she grew anxious or excessively concerned."

"Was the cause ever identified?" I asked.

"Not with any certainty. She saw several physicians over the years. One concluded that her heart was defective, another that the blood supply to her brain was periodically interrupted. Still others put forward opinions that were less conventional."

I glanced at my friend and saw understanding written on his face. After several more questions and a short but friendly conversation we thanked Miss Crenthorpe and left. We had walked almost to the edge of Sir James' estate when I broke the silence between us.

"I cannot see that we learned much Holmes, except for a little of Mrs Feldeane's life that seems unconnected to our investigation."

"Much to the contrary, old friend. Until now the purpose of the apparition had eluded me, but no more. As each piece of the puzzle presents itself, the picture becomes clearer."

He then launched into a detailed description of some of the habits of the birds who flittered among the trees around us, which I knew was his way of deflecting more of my questions. When we reached Darkly Grange we were ushered into the sitting-room by Meluish, to find Sir James awaiting us.

"Gentlemen," he said as we entered, "I have good news. A telegram from Inspector Soames has arrived, in advance of his intended visit tomorrow morning. It seems the fellow who killed poor Mrs Feldeane and her son has been arrested in Braintree. Perhaps I misjudged the inspector, after all."

Holmes accepted a glass of port as I had done, and we settled ourselves in comfortable armchairs.

"I regret that I am unable to agree, Sir James. However, the inspector's visit will be most timely, since I expect to have the real villain in readiness for him by then."

"Are you certain, Mr Holmes?" our host put down his glass wearing an incredulous expression.

"There can be no doubt of it."

"But that means that this poor fellow who Soames has arrested is innocent."

Holmes nodded. "He is, in fact, the second innocent to suffer in this affair."

"Who is the other unfortunate then?" I enquired.

"The maid who you dismissed for stealing food, Sir James. She was quite blameless."

The dermatologist appeared totally shocked. He attempted a few words, but then gave up and drained his glass before he was able to respond.

"I am not usually such a poor judge of character. Again I ask if you are confident in your conclusions."

"They are simple enough to verify. I take it that your cook is at present engaged in preparing luncheon?"

"Of course. It will be served in less than an hour."

"If you will summon her, I will not detain her for long."

"Very well." Sir James rang for Melhuish, who was promptly despatched to the kitchen. After a few minutes a stout but pleasant woman appeared, with all the indications of one who is both hot and busy.

"You called for me, Sir James?" She said, with respect.

"Yes, Martha. Pray answer a question or two from Mr Holmes."

She turned to us, and Holmes spoke in a kindly voice.

"Pray do not be alarmed, Martha. You are aware that the maid, Alice, was dismissed for stealing food?"

"Yes sir."

"But since then, is food still disappearing?"

She looked nervously at Sir James, then at the carpet at her feet. "It is. Sir."

"Then why have you not reported this?"

"I did not wish to be blamed sir, as Alice was."

"You need have no fear, Martha," Sir James said then. "It appears I have some restitution to make, since I have punished an innocent girl."

Our host was unusually quiet during luncheon, doubtlessly regretting his recent treatment of Alice or speculating who was likely the guilty party. When the meal was over he called for the landau to take us to Mortley Manor. The conversation during the journey was almost exclusively between Sir James and myself. Holmes sat beside me brooding, or perhaps reviewing the facts he had gleaned from his observations. He was oblivious, I knew of old, to the beauty and freshness of the fields, flowers and trees around us.

Quite suddenly, our driver turned our conveyance into a grove of tall oaks. These screened out the afternoon sunlight, so that the only illumination was from the remaining narrow strip of sky directly overhead. I saw deer watching us cautiously from concealment, and squirrels scampering along leafy branches. Further afield, sheep were dotted about the landscape.

The landau came to rest before a sturdy door that opened at once. A tall man, remarkably young, I thought, to occupy his position, stood waiting. We alighted and Sir James approached him.

"Good afternoon, Farquar. I have brought these gentlemen, who share the interest of your master and myself, here to see his collection. If you would be so good as to announce us."

The butler frowned. "I can do nothing but apologise, sir. The master is away."

"I am surprised. Do you know when he will return?"

"He did not say, he indicated only that he could be away for a week at most."

I glanced at Holmes, and saw an expression that told me that he had anticipated this.

"Did he mention his intended destination?" asked Sir James.

"Not to me, sir," Farquar adopted a mildly conspiratorial tone, "but I did chance to hear him mention to the cook that he had some legal business to attend to. He did not say where, however."

"I understand," our host said. "Look, will you allow us to see Erasmus' collection in his absence? I am quite certain that he would raise no objection."

Farquar hesitated.

"It would be a pity to have come so far to see such splendid work, only to be disappointed," my friend remarked sadly.

The butler made his decision, smiling. "I am sure the master would be glad to accommodate you gentlemen. Please come in. I will take you to the gallery."

In contrast to Sir James' collection, the portraits here were displayed openly along a wide corridor. Holmes peered at each as we passed.

"Many of these are ancestral, as are your own, Sir James. Some of the subjects are the same." He reached the end of a long display, and stood thoughtfully. "Others are unknown to me. Pray indicate the likeness of your brother, Gilbert."

Sir James stood back and looked along the wall and back, then did so again. "I cannot see it, Mr Holmes. I imagine that Erasmus has sent it away for restoration or cleaning."

"Yes, of course. It must be that."

We spent a further forty minutes in the gallery, during which my friend surprised me by putting his face to the wall several times in order to see beneath the ornate frames. When we were once more aboard the landau, the driver, who was noticeably less talkative than on our arrival, set off at once.

Holmes said nothing, but I detected an air of satisfaction about him as the green fields again sped by. I sensed Sir James' expectancy increase, as did my own, until he could bear the silence no longer.

"Well, Mr Holmes, did you learn anything from our visit?"

"Nothing that I did not expect to find, Sir James."

"Such a pity that your cousin was absent," I remarked to our host.

Holmes smiled faintly. "I would have been surprised to find him in residence."

"He did not inform me of his intention to be away." Sir James looked perplexed at Holmes' remark, but did not pursue it. "What will you do now?"

Holmes consulted his pocket-watch. "I must examine the second floor of Darkly Grange with your permission, Sir James. There is, I think, time enough for that before dinner."

So it was that, half an hour or so later, Holmes and I stood alone in a dusty corridor.

"You will see, Watson, that the floor tells us of recent habitation here, although some effort has been made to conceal the footprints in the dust. Now," he produced a measuring-tape from his pocket, "if we count nine rooms from the right, or the left as it was when viewed from the garden, we will see what can be learned."

He then sank to his knees and crawled four doors to the left of the selected position, and then four to the right, always measuring the distance between them. Finally, he got to his feet and put away the tape before brushing the dust from his clothes.

"What have you discovered?" I enquired, having noted that the open doors revealed that the rooms were empty.

"It really was most skilfully done," he said after a moment. "The intricate pattern all along the walls within is an effective additional concealment. I imagine the original intention was to hide priests from the wrath of reigning monarchs who disagreed with the religion of this household."

"You are referring to some concealed space?"

He pointed to the skirting-board. "You see, Watson, the width of every window is slightly less than that of its neighbour. This is so much so that, at this point, there is sufficient left-over space for another narrow room. There is no indication of that from here, but an additional window looks out upon the garden."

"If you are correct, Holmes, then where is the entrance to this hidden chamber?"

He went into the rooms at either side of the chosen position and rapped upon the walls. After a moment he returned.

"Somewhere nearby is a sliding panel or trapdoor. It must be of substantial construction, since testing the walls brings no result. However, the time has arrived for dinner, I think. Sir James will be curious as to our absence."

In fact, both Sir James and I said very little throughout an excellent dinner of locally-caught bream, and I considered that this was because some sort of explanation from Holmes was expected but not forthcoming. I knew that it was my friend's custom not to reveal his conclusions until he was ready, but Sir James had no such familiarity with him. Holmes seemed to sense this, and after the dessert of strawberries and cream was served he spoke to our host in a calming voice.

"Have no fear, Sir James. I confidently expect to put this matter to rights before another day dawns. You may depend upon it."

Sir James nodded agreeably, doubtlessly remembering from his previous encounter that Holmes was invariably as good as his word. From that moment the atmosphere seemed to lighten somewhat, and after coffee we sat for a while smoking cigarettes. The evening drew on until midnight was little more than an hour away, and it had long been dark before we finally rose to retire.

The servants had extinguished most of the lights as we approached our rooms. I had my hand on the door-handle, but Holmes shook his head.

"Not for us yet, Watson. We have work to do."

I followed him to the stairs and we crept to the second floor. Our footfalls made no noise as we groped our way to our earlier position and waited silently in the darkness.

On many of our previous adventures, I have accompanied my friend on a vigil such as faced us now. Because of the darkness and silence, and much against my will, these interludes are a constant fight against falling asleep. The cramp that sets into my war wound from long immobility is a difficulty also. Holmes, however, always appears immune from both. His stillness is that of a statue, and his breathing I cannot hear. When he speaks it is in the lightest whisper, and very infrequently.

We were able to seat ourselves upon the long empty chest that stood opposite the yawning darkness of the open doors. I sensed that Holmes was fully alert and constantly shifting his attention from one room to the next. By my estimation at least an hour had passed, during which the only sounds had been the faint ringing of a bell that I presumed emanated from a distant monastery or convent, and an occasional scuttling of rats somewhere within the house. I found myself battling against a persistent drowsiness, until I was startled by words spoken so quietly that they were hardly more than an intake of breath.

"Did you hear it, Watson? It came from the room on your right."

I had heard nothing, but Holmes' sharp ears had not failed him. Seconds later, I heard a scraping noise, as of an ill-fitting door opening.

"Keep your hand on your weapon," he whispered then. He rose and entered the room like a shifting shadow, and I followed.

An entire section of the wall we faced moved slowly and horizontally out of sight. The cavity exposed was almost the height of the room, and the dim glow from within was extinguished immediately. We stood still and silent, our weapons drawn as a vague figure stepped out and moved unknowingly towards us. Holmes opened his dark lantern, startling the man who was revealed.

"Make no attempt to escape," my friend commanded, "we are both armed.

The figure was still at once, but made no sound.

"Watson, enter the secret room and light the oil lamp that our friend here extinguished a moment ago, then tell me what you see in there."

I complied at once. The lamp was easily found atop a stool near the entrance. I lit it with a vesper and was at once surprised, as the room was of much greater size than I had imagined.

"There is dust everywhere," I began, "but I see the remains of several meals scattered across the floor together with wine bottles that appear to be full of water. A portrait is propped against the wall near the window." I held up the lamp. "The section of wall that formed the concealed entrance is of solid wood, and was manipulated by a system of pulleys. Oil has been applied recently."

"That will do, old fellow. I seem to have been correct in my suppositions, although there is still much to learn from this man. Come out of there and we will find a more convenient place to question him."

I left that evil-smelling place and held our prisoner at gunpoint while Holmes secured his hands with police handcuffs. Descending to the ground floor was slow and uncertain, I preceded the restrained man and Holmes held his revolver at the ready behind him.

"In here." Holmes opened a heavy door in the corridor. It led into a small room that contained nothing but an ornate table and three chairs. I realised that he must have foreseen the situation and possibly described it to Sir James. I guarded our prisoner while Holmes lit two oil lamps and extinguished his dark lantern.

"Sit there, Mr Erasmus Bartley." Holmes directed him to the single stiff-backed chair positioned on one side of the table, as we took our seats opposite. "My name is Sherlock Holmes. I am a consulting detective and my companion is Doctor John Watson."

"He is Sir James' cousin?" I queried with astonishment.

"Who else could he be, Watson, when everything is considered? When I learn that the tormentor and murderer of Mrs Feldeane knows of the concealed room in this house, is familiar with its history and her former engagement to Sir James' brother and is in possession of a portrait of him, what other conclusion can there be?" He placed his weapon upon the table, but near his hand, and looked sternly at our prisoner.

"Since you have spoken not a word since we encountered you emerging from your hiding place, I presume you intend to maintain your silence?"

Mr Bartley said nothing and avoided Holmes' steely stare, fixing his eyes upon the table-top.

"Very well then, since you will reveal nothing of this affair, I will relate it to you as I see it. You are at liberty to correct me, if I stray from the truth."

Holmes and I glanced at each other. Our prisoner did not move.

"Firstly, you knew of the forthcoming garden party well in advance," Holmes began, "although it was not your custom to attend. You had made your plans. I am aware that you were responsible for the death of Rowens, Sir James' butler, though I have yet to discover how. You then recommended Courtney, who was yourself in disguise, to replace him."

"How is that possible?" I asked.

Holmes allowed himself a brief smile. "Observe the traces of theatrical make-up remaining on Mr Bartley's face, Watson. He has had no opportunity to remove them, and you have surely noticed that his clothes are those of a butler. You will recall Sir James mentioning that his cousin once joined a circus, where he doubtlessly learned the art of changing his facial appearance."

"He also impersonated Mrs Feldeane's former fiance, Mr Gilbert Saunders, then?" I ventured.

"Not so, old friend. Having poisoned the wine that he knew she would drink, he realised that he had no means of determining *when* she would take it. The delicate balance of her health was known to him. He therefore arranged for an appearance of her former fiance to induce a seizure such as she suffered when shocked or suddenly startled. This was achieved by a momentary display of Mr Gilbert's portrait at the window, but he was not quite quick enough in removing it since Sir James also glimpsed the image."

I stared hard at Erasmus Bartley. "That was callous, sir. I hope you are now suitably ashamed." The obvious question then occurred to me. "But why was it necessary to kill Mrs Feldeane and her son? What harm could they have done to you?"

He made no response, other than to lower his head further so that only his crown was visible to us.

"The answer to that question is a simple one," Holmes explained. "You will recall that Sir James stated that his guests were mostly from afar. Mrs Feldeane and her son then, were the only ones likely to recognise 'Courtney' as, in truth, his cousin."

"And the portrait was from his collection at Mortley Manor, and the true reason for our visit there," I realised.

"Precisely. He was careful enough not to leave an empty space among his pictures upon the wall, but by looking beneath them I saw marks suggesting that one had recently replaced a portrait of a slightly smaller size. That, and the fact that he had been absent for a while, confirmed the supposition that I had formed."

"But," I objected, "all this means that three people have died in order to allow and preserve this man's impersonation of a butler in his cousin's house. Holmes, what can be the reason behind this?"

"Have you not realised yet? It is the Cezanne. Sir James would not sell it, so his cousin devised a rather elaborate means to obtain its possession."

Erasmus Bartley raised his head, and stared at us with eyes that held a strange expression. His blunt, unshaven features held no hint of fear or regret, but a crafty smile lingered upon his lips.

"I have always known," he began in a hoarse and indifferent voice, "that it was likely that the hangman would end my life." He stared directly at Holmes. "You, sir, are a man of some ability, to have reconstructed my actions and intentions with such accuracy. As you may know, I never married, for that would have satisfied neither of the two passions that have always dominated me. The first, as you have deduced, is art. I crave for the exquisite works of the Masters as some men crave gold, and have pursued their possession with no less determination. In my home there are far more examples than those you have seen, and well hidden. Oh yes, I have stolen, blackmailed and killed to acquire those sources of satisfaction and fulfilment. Some would refer to my enthusiasm as obsessive. I consider it as of no account that it is my cousin who is the owner of that wonderful portrait. Such an accident of birth in no way alters my intent. I would have taken the Cezanne without harm to him or the others hereabouts if that were possible, but otherwise….."

"You would have murdered your cousin?" I asked as he paused.

"Is that not your second passion?" enquired Holmes. "Murder?"

The furtive expression intensified. "The killing of my fellow man, or woman, on occasion? Yes, it has always filled me with a joy and satisfaction that I could not describe to you. As a young man I joined a circus because I felt the county police were getting close to discovering that I was responsible for several deaths that occurred in the area, and of course my travels as a clown or acrobat provided many opportunities abroad. As for Rowens, who you were concerned about, a fine needle inserted in the base of his skull produced his unexpected demise rather more quickly than I would have liked, but then it was experimental. I always enjoyed trying new methods, especially those of my own invention." He raised his manacled hands to brush away a lock of lank hair. "But, make no mistake, gentlemen, I have suffered for my extravagances. Awaiting my chance in that hidden room that I had known about since a childhood exploration, breathing the foul air and creeping about this place to take food from the kitchen in the early hours was not the least of it. But it was necessary, and but for you I would have taken a prize to be the pinnacle of my collection."

I was about to remark that the future held for him, at best, the remainder of his life in an asylum, when the door opened. Our heads turned to see Sir James, wearing a dressing-gown over his nightshirt and holding a lantern, framed in the entrance.

"Mr Holmes, I could not sleep so...." He stopped abruptly as he saw our prisoner. "Good heavens! Erasmus, why are you restrained" Then the truth of the situation became obvious to him, and he groaned heavily. "Oh, my God, no."

"I regret, Sir James, that this is indeed the outcome of my investigation," my friend replied. "When he arrives, Inspector Soames will have little to do, other than make the arrest and accompany Mr Bartley to the local police station. As for the African prospector that Mrs Feldeane and yourself glimpsed at the window that day, I am afraid that he remains lost to you."

The Adventure of the Cheerful Prisoner

Some of Holmes most interesting cases came to him through Mycroft' – from "The Greek Interpreter".

The exact function among the procedures of Whitehall of Sherlock Holmes' elder brother was always a mystery to me and, I suspect to a lesser extent, to Holmes himself. It was always apparent that he commanded great respect and had great power within his circle of colleagues, and even my friend usually treated him with some reverence. Until my meeting with him during the affair involving Mister Kratides which I have related elsewhere, I was completely ignorant of his existence, but since that time his hand or his presence has featured often in our enquiries and investigations.

"I take it, Holmes, that you expect no clients today, since you ate your breakfast in such a leisurely fashion," I said as our plates were cleared away one early summer morning.

This was an easy observation, since his usual behaviour of immediately leaping from the table on the completion of our meal to hurriedly retrieve our hats and coats while displaying extreme eagerness to embark upon an enquiry was noticeably altered. Today he had slowly consumed both the last of his toast and his final cup of coffee whilst staring absently and silently into space, not moving from his chair.

On hearing my words, he seemed to come to himself. "You are quite correct, Watson. I despatched a telegram to Gregson yesterday, with sufficient evidence to put Ambrill in the dock. I have nothing else on hand, at the moment."

"And I have reason to expect few patients this morning, although Manderson will arrive later to serve as locum for a day or two. I prescribe a short holiday for both of us, since we have shown symptoms of excessive weariness lately. What do you say to a change – sea air or open spaces?"

I saw that my suggestion did not sit well with Holmes. His expression showed no enthusiasm for adopting a different scene and a slower pace, even for a short while. I remembered his response to similar proposals on previous occasions, and reflected that I should have felt no surprise.

"If you need to travel, Watson, then pray do so. As for me, I feel no need to leave the capital. Who knows what new problems might present themselves and remain without attention, if I am absent?"

"Holmes!" I exclaimed. "You really must keep in mind that there is more in life than work. I understand that this is your consuming interest and that it is your means of survival but, need I remind you, you have been brought close to nervous exhaustion before now, by over-exertion."

"I have explained to you before, my need for almost constant mental stimulation. Without it my existence is colourless and stagnant. If you wish to leave Baker Street for a holiday then do what you must, but do not include me in your plans. I have no doubt that you will encounter others who will become your temporary companions, for you are a far more sociable fellow than I."

It was thus clear to me that, if I were to undertake such a journey, it would be alone.

Nevertheless, I decided on one more attempt to cause him to change his mind.

"Do you not recall the other occasions when we have returned here refreshed and like new men? I merely wished to….." I was interrupted by the peal of the door-bell and Holmes brightened instantly.

"Our immediate future may have been decided for us," he speculated. "Or mine, at least."

We listened in silence as we waited for our good landlady to answer the door. The cries of barrow-boys and the sounds of passing hansoms drifted up to us through the half-open window as we heard the door close after a few moments. I believe that we had both concluded, because of the light tread upon the stairs which we recognised as Mrs Hudson's alone, that our visitor was not a new client but had arrived with a message.

At the sound of a knock on our door, Holmes called for our landlady to enter. She presented him with a telegram upon a polished tray, which he accepted with thanks. He had torn open the yellow envelope before the door closed behind her, and I leaned forward in my chair expectantly.

"From Mycroft," he informed me, holding the message up to the light. "He asks that we visit him in Whitehall, at ten. Apparently, it is an urgent matter."

I rose. "I will get our hats and coats."

"But what of your holiday?"

"He specified both of us, according to your narration. I did not say I intended to depart this morning."

Not long after, a hansom pulled by a sprightly young colt deposited us near the office of Holmes' elder brother with a few minutes to spare.

As on previous occasions, a uniformed aide awaited us. He led us through a maze of corridors, marching stiffly and saying nothing since his formal greeting. At last we entered a short passageway, with but three anonymous doors before us. Our companion knocked upon the second of these, and I heard a muffled response from within. He opened the door and stood aside to admit us, announcing us in a toneless voice.

Mycroft Holmes looked up from his desk as the door was closed behind us. I saw at once that he had changed little. He struggled to raise his bulk from his chair.

"Sherlock, Doctor Watson! How good to see you. Do come and sit down, I think you will find the chairs comfortable. Would you care for tea?"

"I think not, thank you Mycroft." My friend answered for both of us. "I would be grateful if you would tell us why we have been summoned with such urgency."

Our host lowered himself back into his chair. The leather creaked as he adjusted his position.

"A problem has arisen, involving a colleague who has worked closely with me for some time. I would rather someone outside my department look into it, since this individual would be previously unknown to them and their judgement therefore, would not be coloured by any familiarity."

"To whom are you referring?" Holmes asked.

"His name is Mr Matthew Faber. He has acted as my liaison with many of our people in Germany and elsewhere for a good while now, and it was something of a shock to discover that his loyalty appears to be in question."

"I have not heard of the man. But then, that is as it should be."

"Quite. Another of my people, Mr Thomas Ollshaw, who knows Faber well, holds a similar position here, and it was he who informed me that news of a succession of incidents that we shall refer to as 'The Biesdorf Affair' had filtered back to him from one of his informants in Berlin."

"This, I presume, was a matter with details thought to be known only to Mr Faber and yourself,"

"You are perceptive as always, Sherlock. That is indeed the case. Any knowledge of the Biesdorf business that exists in Germany must have originated from Faber. I confess to being confounded by both the man's actions and his reasons for them. I summoned both he and Ollshaw at once, but Faber would say nothing."

"Is he married?" I enquired, as a possibility occurred to me.

"Yes, Doctor. He and his wife live in Highgate." Mycroft's tone told me that he considered my question to be irrelevant, and I abandoned the thought.

"Where is he now?" Holmes asked. He would, I knew, have already formed some sort of supposition.

"At Ollshaw's suggestion, I had Faber placed under guard and later transported to Dartmoor Prison. We agreed that it was better he should leave the capital for a place where any of his German contacts, if indeed he has any, would have great difficulty in obtaining more information from him."

"You have doubts about his guilt, then?"

"Ah, Sherlock, you concluded that because I said 'if he has any'."

"Precisely. I saw at once that you find it difficult to believe that you could have misjudged Faber so, after a considerable time of working with him closely."

Mycroft nodded. "There is something here that strikes a false note. I am involved at present in negotiations concerning the Trieste agreement, so I have not the time to go into this further. I thought you might be prepared to assist me...."

The question was left hanging in the air.

"Very well," Holmes answered after a few moments had passed.

Mycroft's expression altered slightly. I took this to be a sign of relief.

"Excellent. I have prepared the answers to any questions you might have as to details, addresses and so forth." He slid a folded paper across the desk and my friend accepted it. "Where will you begin?"

Holmes gave his brother a look that told me he felt mildly insulted.

"Why, at Princetown of course. I believe it to be the site of Dartmoor prison?"

"You wish to interview Faber at the outset. I would have been surprised had you suggested otherwise. The temporary prison governor, I understand, is Mr William Crout, who occupies the position because of the illness of his superior. I will see that he is notified to expect you. Naturally, you will be departing for Devonshire, this morning?"

"Watson and I will be departing for Devonshire by either the mid-day or afternoon train," Holmes corrected. "We have some minor affairs to settle and our bags to pack."

"Of course," Mycroft scowled impatiently. "I look forward to your report."

Holmes said not a word until we were settled in a hansom and well on our way back to Baker Street. I could sense his anger.

"Were you planning to spend the day otherwise?" I asked him as our conveyance turned sharply to avoid an urchin who scuttled across the road. "Clearly, the interview with your brother has perturbed you."

"Not at all," he answered in a restrained voice. "It is Mycroft's assumption that he can treat me as one of his lackeys that infuriates me. He presumes on our brotherly relationship too much. 'I look forward to your report,' indeed. He has done this before now, despite my protestations."

I saw that it would be as well to shift the conversation.

"I wonder if this man Faber could be innocent," I said.

"There must be reason to suppose so, or my brother would not concern himself with the man's fate. Hopefully our investigation will indicate the truth."

We arrived at our lodgings shortly afterwards, and to my astonishment I discovered that it was already almost time for luncheon. Mrs Hudson served a satisfying meal of roast pork followed by apple pie, but Holmes ate little.

When our plates had been cleared and the coffee pot emptied we hurriedly packed our travelling cases.

"It is hardly worth the trouble for one night," Holmes remarked. "Normally I would have taken no more than a clean collar and a toothbrush, but I feel an uncertainty about this. If events take an unexpected turn, then our stay may be extended."

Having made our preparations, we summoned a passing cab for the short journey to Waterloo Station. I waited on the platform while

Holmes procured our tickets, and the early afternoon train arrived on time.

With the next five or six hours before us, I seized the opportunity to persuade my friend to relate one of his past cases, having recognised his mood as one most likely to allow this. After a reluctant few minutes he agreed, and as the grimy suburbs of London passed us by I was privileged to hear the tale of Miss Barbara Forsythe and the African tinker – one of his cases from his time in Montague Street.

Presently his revelation came to a close, and he lapsed into a morose state and then into silence. I was eventually lulled into sleep by the motion of the train and awoke, astonished at the length of my unintended slumber, to see him staring unseeingly in my direction, yet far away amidst his own thoughts.

A glance at the passing scenery was enough to tell me that we were now in Devonshire. The soil was now of a deeper, ruddy colour and the grass and trees were luxuriant. Fields of cattle and sheep, interrupted by stone cottages, were plentiful among the rolling hills. After a while the land took on a more level but wilder appearance, and I knew from of old that we were nearing the moor.

We left the train at Oakhampton Station, and soon enlisted the services of an elderly man who had used his cart to deliver several cages of racing pigeons to await a later train.

When Holmes informed him of our intended destination he gave us a sharp look, but bid us board his conveyance nevertheless. He spoke little during the journey, except to point out the way to various villages and warn us of the danger of our surroundings.

This, I felt, was quite unnecessary. At the moment when we reached the point where the outskirts of the village gave way to that sinister and deserted waste, all that I had felt during our previous adventure of some years ago came flooding back to me. As the cart bumped over a winding track that must have seen centuries of wheeled traffic I recalled the mysterious and remote atmosphere that hung heavily over the place, the eerie sounds and strange movements among the ferns and bracken that had been known to terrify superstitious folk and the noisy streams that flowed beneath small stony bridges.

I dwelt on such thoughts for some little time while Holmes rode in silence, perhaps reminiscing also.

I had resolved to put past impressions out of my mind, and to concentrate on our present purpose when he suddenly pointed ahead.

"There, Watson. A structure as unprepossessing as that can be nothing else but a prison, surely."

Our driver confirmed that this was indeed the place we sought, a large and dull structure that already seemed to me to be surrounded by gloom. We alighted, paid the man and watched the cart out of sight, before Holmes struck the great doors with his fist and shouted to announce our arrival.

We were admitted at once, and on stating our names and purpose led along a cheerless stone-flagged corridor to be shown into an office containing a battered desk and several badly worn chairs. Pictures of our Queen and stern-looking men who I presumed were past governors adorned the walls, and the place had the chill of the grave about it.

The middle-aged man behind the desk was apparently unaffected. He rose and greeted us.

"Good evening, gentlemen. I trust your journey was pleasant. I am William Crout, governor here until my superior regains his health."

We introduced ourselves, and his face brightened.

"We have heard of you here of course, Mr Holmes, but I was surprised to receive a telegram from Whitehall, especially in connection with the prisoner Matthew Faber."

"Is he then, in some way different?"

Mr Crout pulled at his moustache, as if momentarily at a loss for words.

"Well, you see, it's like this, sirs. To begin with, we haven't been told what the man has done, nor any details of his trial. The instructions we received were simply to confine him while waiting for further orders. That's odd in itself, but the behaviour of the man has me baffled."

"He has tried to escape?" I ventured.

"No, Doctor, the very opposite. We're used to prisoners trying to get out from time to time, using various schemes they've invented, though few of them get very far. But this man, in my experience at least, is like no other. Ever since he was brought here he has shown every sign of contentment and happiness. He sings to himself in his cell, jokes with the guards who take him his food and laughs a lot." The temporary governor scratched his head. "I really cannot make any sense of it."

"Intriguing," said Holmes. "We were asked to interview him regarding his behaviour in Whitehall, in the course of his employment."

I noticed that my friend spoke in vague terms, mentioning nothing that Mr Crout could not easily have deduced for himself.

"Perhaps then, you will more fortunate than myself and others. It may be that you can get him to confide why he is in such remarkably good spirits in a place where it is usual to experience extreme melancholia." He raised his stocky form from his chair. "Come, gentlemen, we will see him now."

He led us from the room and a guard joined us in a walk along empty corridors. We entered several where our passage was accompanied by shouts from behind the barred doors, together with appeals and oaths. Often, implements were rattled against the bars. The guard retaliated with harsh warnings, and the noise ceased quickly.

Our little procession came to an abrupt halt before a door that was identical with its neighbours. The guard produced keys and selected one which opened the cell.

We looked in to see a smiling young man look up from a tattered book.

"I take it you would prefer to interview the prisoner alone?" Mr Crout enquired.

"If you would be so kind," Holmes replied.

"Then I will return to my office. Martland here will station himself nearby so that you can call when you wish to leave. I will see you presently, gentlemen, and I wish you success."

With that, both prison officials turned and left before the cell door was closed behind us.

Matthew Faber put down his book and got to his feet. He approached Holmes and shook his hand vigorously.

"Did Mr Mycroft send you?" he asked expectantly.

"Indeed he did."

"What is his message for me. Tell me quickly."

Holmes appeared faintly puzzled. "We are to discuss the circumstances surrounding your imprisonment."

"But he instructed me to...." His pleasant manner vanished, and his expression became furtive. "Wait! This is a test. I have nothing to say to you gentlemen. You may tell Mr Mycroft that."

"He suspects that the circumstances may have been incorrectly understood. We merely wish you to explain your actions, if indeed they were yours, that brought about the accusation."

"I repeat, I can tell you nothing."

"I am a doctor," I explained. "I would like to know if you have been injured, or if your health is suffering since your incarceration."

"There is no need to concern yourself, sir. No misfortune has befallen me, and I have not been brutalised. Nothing here has disagreed with me. I have endured worse, before now."

He then fell silent, and no amount of questioning or encouragement would dissuade him from his course. Holmes regarded him thoughtfully as I made further attempts to learn something without success.

"Very well." Holmes approached the door and I followed. He turned to the prisoner. "Have you anything that you wish me to tell Mycroft?"

Faber shook his head but then relented, changing his demeanour and saying quickly. "But if I might beg a favour. Could I prevail upon you to visit my wife, my Iris? Please inform her that I am well and in no danger. When this is over I will be home."

All joviality was gone, replaced by concern.

"It will be attended to," Holmes answered, before calling for the guard.

Martland escorted us back to Mr Crout's office. The temporary governor now looked tired.

"Well, gentlemen, were you able to learn anything? He enquired hopefully.

"Nothing," Holmes admitted, "except that he seems to be convinced that his release is imminent. That, I would think, explains his unusual pleasantness. He believes that whatever he is accused of will be found to be false and the charge dropped. I regret that I can enlighten you no further."

"That at least explains his unusual response to incarceration." Mr Crout consulted his pocket-watch. "But how will you gentlemen return to the capital? By now it will be dark outside, and it is as well not to be abroad hereabouts. As you must have seen, Princetown is a small community, but we do have a respectable inn that will be able to put you up for the night. If you turn right as you leave, into the main street and past the church, you will come to The Flag and Anchor, a public house of local repute." He struggled to his feet as before and shook both our hands. "Goodbye, gentlemen. I wish you a safe journey tomorrow."

We left that grim place to discover that a light mist had appeared. As we walked the short distance through the darkness our previous encounters on the moor again came back to me. I dismissed them from my mind as we approached the ill-lit main street and, having passed a few darkened shops, the Post Office and the church, soon found the inn. We had not eaten since luncheon and hunger pangs were making themselves felt. Holmes, of course, showed no signs of discomfort. Nevertheless, we enjoyed a fine meal of roast chicken and spent the evening with pints of the landlord's best beer. A few local people gave us queer looks but no one approached or spoke to us. Holmes commented that such distrust was common in rural or isolated communities, and we retired to our rooms early. I lay listening to the faint conversation and occasional laughter from below, which ceased before long. I heard the landlord slamming home the bolts on the front door, after which I fell asleep in absolute silence.

After a breakfast of local ham and eggs, Holmes asked the landlord about transportation to the station. A man with a cart appeared soon after, and earned himself a generous tip as, carrying our meagre luggage, we left him near Oakhampton Station.

Holmes and I had spoken little about our visit to Mr Matthew Faber. As we began the journey back to London he was silent for a while, and I was about to make a remark when he ended his reverie abruptly.

"There is something more here, Watson," he said suddenly.

"You mean regarding Mr Faber?"

"I do. Two things stand out. The first is that he expected some message from Mycroft, yet resisted further conversation upon learning that we were there to discover more about his predicament. He seemed to believe that our presence was for some sort of testing of him."

"To determine the truth of something he had previously stated, perhaps?"

"That is of course possible, but I am further disturbed by his remark when he made the request concerning his wife. As you recall, he said, *When this is over.* That suggests that he is aware of the duration of this affair, and that he is unashamed of his conduct. I believe that, either Mycroft has been deceived, or he is withholding some aspect from us."

"Are we to visit your brother, perhaps after lunch?"

"I think not. I may consult him later. This afternoon, I think we will keep my promise to Mr Faber."

The remainder of the journey passed swiftly, because Holmes embarked on a tirade about the Trojan War, which interested me because I had read something of it. On our arrival at Waterloo, a hansom swiftly presented itself, and so we returned to our lodgings in time to prevail upon Mrs Hudson for a late luncheon.

As always, she made no complaint, and I had the impression that she had exercised that unerring instinct that she seemed to possess regarding our departures and arrivals. A good meal of fresh trout was served long before I could have reasonably expected it to appear. When it was over, and I had consumed my dessert alone, Holmes put down his coffee cup and rose from the table.

"When you have ceased your rather excessive feeding habits, Watson, we will make our way to Highgate."

I resisted the temptation to give an acid reply. "You have Mrs Faber's address?"

"Mycroft's written details and instructions are most comprehensive," he said with a scowl.

Less than ten minutes later, we found ourselves in a cab. We left the city on a road that was soon surrounded by green fields and farmer's cottages. Presently we approached the outskirts of the district and, after passing a few shops and stables, our driver turned into a pleasant avenue of red-brick houses.

The hansom left us and we peered at the doors before us.

"This could be difficult, Holmes. The houses are not numbered."

He smiled briefly. "So I have observed. However, I would wager that the fifth residence from that rather neglected house to our right is the one that we seek."

"How could you know that?"

"You will recall Mr Faber's appearance. He had managed to make himself presentable, despite his confinement. That suggests that he is a person of order and tidiness. Also, this is not a very affluent part of the district, yet the house that I have indicated presents an immaculate sight, with a flower bed and well-swept path. Mr Faber can doubtlessly afford such maintenance, on the adequate sum that his employment provides."

I was by no means convinced of the accuracy of my friend's deductions, until the door was answered by a young woman of startling beauty. She looked at us uncomprehendingly at first, then it must have dawned on her that we must have some connection with her husband's situation and she gave a thin smile as she bade us enter.

We found ourselves in a pleasant living room, well decorated and with new furniture and several large pots containing flourishing aspidistras. As expected, Mrs Faber wore a concerned look which seemed to me also confused. She wore a plain blue frock and a string of pearls about her neck.

"Gentlemen, I can only hope that you have brought me good news," she began when we were seated. "I have been almost out of my mind with worry. What my Matthew is accused of I cannot tell, but I know him to be a good and honest man. Perhaps you can enlighten me – why was he suddenly arrested and transported to

Dartmoor Prison? That is the only information I have received regarding his fate."

"We are here," Holmes answered, "first to convey to you a message from your husband. He wants you to know that he is well and optimistic about an early release. The other news we have for you is that there is thought to be some doubt about his guilt. Forgive me for not introducing ourselves. I am Sherlock Holmes, and my companion is Doctor John Watson. We are investigating the circumstances surrounding your husband's arrest, in the hope that the truth may be brought to light. To that end, will you permit us to ask questions that may clear things up?"

She sat forward anxiously in her chair. "Of course! I would do anything to save him."

"Thank you." Holmes sat upright, his eyes never leaving her. "Please tell us, what you know of your husband's work."

"Very little. I am aware that his employment is in a building in Whitehall, but little else. His work is never discussed between us, and he discourages references to it. I formed the impression that he is concerned with overseas trade."

"Quite so. Do you know of any incident, however small, that could explain his arrest. Pray think carefully, in terms of now and however long he has held his present position."

"There is nothing," she replied without hesitation. "We are close, anything untoward would have affected Matthew, and I would have known."

Holmes nodded. "It is necessary then, to ask you but one more question. Are you acquainted with a colleague of Mr Faber's, a man called Thomas Ollshaw?"

"Why yes, Matthew has known him for years." She twirled a stray lock of dark hair around a finger, remembering. "He and his wife used to visit here often, as we did to their home. Sadly his wife passed away about two years ago, even more so because their union was short. In fact, Mr Holmes, had you arrived half an hour earlier, you would have met him. He has been here several times since this trouble began. He is a kind and sympathetic man."

"Thank you for your valuable assistance," my friend concluded. "I am certain that things will be put right before long."

I put away my note-book, the writings therein my only contribution to the proceedings, and we took our leave.

We came upon Highgate High Street as a hansom deposited two young ladies near a milliner's shop, and procured it immediately. After stating our destination Holmes was initially silent, and I was giving consideration to what we had learned.

He was staring at the passing trees, and the fields of cows and sheep, when I asked him:

"Holmes, do you believe Mr Faber to be guilty? Your brother indicated that the charge was a serious one. Were this a time of war he would undoubtedly meet the hangman if convicted. At best, he would be imprisoned for many years."

"I should be surprised if he is guilty of anything. However, I shall be able to confirm this when we meet Mr Ollshaw tomorrow. As it will be Sunday, we should find him at home."

When our dinner, a bulging steak and ale pie followed by stewed apple, was consumed, we settled into our usual chairs. Both Holmes and I were weary from the day's exertions, and after less conversation than was our custom for evenings, we retired. I passed a fitful night. An image of Mrs Faber in complete distress on learning of her husband's guilt would not leave me, despite Holmes' assurance.

The kippers at breakfast were excellent, and we both ate with relish. Holmes surprised me by appearing to be in no hurry. He sipped his coffee slowly and seemed to be in a jovial mood.

When I asked him about his good spirits, he gave a thin smile and said:

"What would you think are the main reasons why crimes are committed, Watson?"

"Money, I suppose. That has been the cause of many in our experience."

"That is correct. What else, would you say?"

I considered for a moment. "Revenge?"

"That too, but there is one other cause that is by no means rare."

"Something driven by lust or emotion, I would think."

"You have it. Passion is a powerful instigator indeed."

"But what has that to do with Mr Faber's alleged crime?" I thought back, to our visit yesterday. "Ah, I see. You suspect that this man Thomas Ollshaw has designs on Mrs Faber."

He nodded. "It is, for the moment, no more than a supposition. It will doubtlessly be proved or disproved when we meet him later."

"Where does Mr Ollshaw live?"

"According to Mycroft's rather extensive notes he resides in Mayfair, which is of course a further indication when applied to the present situation."

"How so, Holmes?"

"We have just discussed the various causes that incline a man towards crime. If Mr Ollshaw is behind this affair it cannot be for profit because he must be quite affluent to live in Mayfair. In addition, Mycroft's notes suggest this. As for revenge, it is unlikely, since Mrs Faber spoke of their long and friendly association. That leaves only passion, so we will see what this morning reveals to us." He then replaced his coffee cup and rose to peer through the half-open window. "Ha! I see that two hansoms have discharged their fares in Baker Street, and their drivers are conversing as they wait for further custom. If we are quick about it, we may be able to interrupt their chatter."

With that he seized our hats and coats. I hurriedly struggled into mine as we descended the stairs at a fast pace. We boarded the nearest cab and in moments were rattling away from our lodgings as soon as Holmes had instructed our driver. As we approached Mayfair our surroundings changed significantly. The houses we passed were larger and clearly more given to style. Long gardens bloomed between the frontages and the pavement, where rows of dwarf pines often defined the border. Our hansom came to rest outside one such residence, a three-storey building with high chimneys, and we alighted.

I paid the cabby and we waited until his conveyance had turned the corner, before setting off along a level path. As we approached the house it took on a formidable look, and the door opened to reveal a uniformed butler who asked us to state our business.

"We are here to see Mr Thomas Ollshaw," Holmes replied.

The butler regarded us suspiciously. "I am not sure if he is at home, sir."

"Pray inform him, if he is, that Mr Sherlock Holmes would like to discuss the future of Mr Matthew Faber with him. Here is my card."

We were left alone for a few minutes. Then the butler returned, stone-faced so that I expected a refusal.

"Please come in, gentlemen," he said tonelessly.

We were shown into a high-ceilinged room decorated in green. Tall windows faced us, with long curtains that were restrained by silken ropes. Before the fireplace stood a tall young man, dressed immaculately in a grey morning-suit. His full beard enclosed thin lips and his eyes, I noticed, were those of a man much grieved.

The butler announced us and withdrew.

"Good morning, gentlemen," Mr Ollshaw began. "My superior, Mr Mycroft Holmes, has often spoken of you both. I am aware that you are taking some part in establishing the guilt or innocence of my colleague, but I cannot see how I can add further to what you must already know."

I noticed that there was no shaking of hands.

When we had accepted his invitation to sit, he pointed questioningly to the bottle of sherry that stood on a tray with glasses near to him. We both declined, as it was still early.

"We have in fact interviewed Mr Faber at Dartmoor Prison," said Holmes. "He was unresponsive to our questions and so it is imperative that we seek information from any other sources to hand. I understand that it was you who first drew my brother's attention to Mr Faber's apparent disloyalty."

"That is correct. One of my informants in Germany reported forthcoming events of which he should have been unaware, doubtlessly gleaned from others in the same trade as himself. According to your brother's subsequent statement to me, only he and Mr Faber were known to be privy to the information. Since Mr Mycroft is naturally above suspicion, it can be no other but Faber who divulged it. I'm afraid this does not look favourable for him."

"No, indeed. I am mystified though, as to his reluctance to speak in his own defence."

"Perhaps he has no defence, or is unable to concoct a sufficiently convincing falsehood. I have known him for a good while, and have never thought of him as a very complicated or deceptive character."

As he spoke, a suggestion of a blush appeared on his face. It struck me as embarrassment, but I could not see why Holmes' statement would cause this.

"Were you at school together?" I enquired.

"He was in the year after me, at Eton."

It seemed as if my friend was losing interest in the conversation, since the focus of his attention appeared to be, not our host, but a framed photographic portrait of a remarkably beautiful woman with long blonde tresses which stood upon a side-table. It struck me for a moment that I had met her, but then I dismissed the notion as highly improbable. After all, had not Mrs Faber mentioned that this lady was deceased?

"My brother taken aback by Mr Faber's actions. I take it that he never heard to remark, or hint in an odd moment, ay anything that could lead you to believe that he harboured any sympathy with the Kaiser?"

"Not at all, but I cannot imagine why he would allow information entrusted to him to be known elsewhere, otherwise."

Holmes nodded. "Well, Mr Ollshaw, you have, after all, cleared up one or two things that had puzzled me about this affair." He rose and I did also. "Thank you for allowing us to intrude upon your Sunday respite."

Shortly afterwards Holmes raised his stick to flag down a passing hansom. He sat with his head upon his chest for a while, as I watched the magnificent homes of the rich give way to lesser residences once Mayfair was left behind.

"Watson," he said suddenly, with the tone of a man awakening from a dream, "I can feel your curiosity. You are wondering why I did not ask many more questions. But why would I, when the confirmation I sought was in front of my eyes, and I had been supplied with indications that I had not even looked for."

"What confirmation? I do not recall….. Ah, the photograph."

"Precisely. You will have realised that the image was that of Mr Ollshaw's departed wife."

"I had surmised so. A woman of great beauty. The effects of her loss were still plain to see on her husband."

"Perhaps, but were you reminded of someone?"

"It did strike me that she looked familiar, but it cannot be."

"True, it cannot. But picture her in your mind, if your memory of the photograph is sufficient. Give her dark hair and make it shorter, so that it curls in at the neck. Take away the over-reddened lips and rouged cheeks."

I closed my eyes and attempted to comply. I strained to bring back the likeness that I had seen for no more than a few minutes. Then Holmes' meaning became clear.

"Good heavens!"

"You see it?"

"She, if her appearance were altered like that, would closely resemble Mrs Faber!"

"Indeed. There then, we have the purpose of Mr Faber's contrived removal which was primarily intended to be from his household, rather than his work."

"Holmes, this is monstrous! Do you think Mr Ollshaw is capable of ruining his friend's career and causing him to be imprisoned, because he desires his wife?"

"I believe that Mrs Ollshaw's death had a greater effect than is usual, upon her husband. But it could be that he had unknowingly transferred his affections to Mrs Faber beforehand, rather than looking upon her as a substitute afterwards. At any rate, we still have work to do since, to Ollshaw, all this has been for nothing unless Mr Faber's absence is made to be permanent."

"But Mr Faber is still in Dartmoor Prison."

"If my hypothesis is sound, then he is safe as long as he remains there. However, our visit to Mr Ollshaw provided the last piece of the puzzle and my case is complete. That is how I know that it is imperative that we return to Dartmoor this afternoon. I recall from my Bradshaw that we have time for a hurried luncheon, but we must without fail catch the afternoon train."

So it was that we incurred Mrs Hudson's displeasure by the speed with which we disposed of an excellent luncheon. No sooner had I pushed away my empty teacup than Holmes, already clad in his ulster and ear-flapped travelling cap, again thrust my own garments towards me. We picked up our bags, hastily packed once more, and secured a hansom after five minutes of my friend's growing impatience.

The afternoon and early evening passed much as before. Holmes had telegraphed ahead to Mr Crout, and so we were expected. The stout doors swung open to admit us, and we were quickly conveyed to the governor's office.

"Gentlemen," the acting governor seemed in a pleasant mood. "I am surprised to see you again, especially so soon. Am I to understand then, that you have made some headway in the peculiar case of the prisoner Faber?"

"I am confident that I can now put matters in their proper perspective," Holmes assured him. "If you would be so good as to allow us to see him again, everything will become clear."

"Very well, but it is fortunate that you did not arrive later."

This I could not understand, but Holmes wore a look of satisfaction, as if his supposition, or part of it, was proven.

"I would think that you have received word from Whitehall."

Mr Crout plucked a telegram from a cluster of papers, and slid it across his desk. "This was delivered an hour ago."

Holmes read it, and passed it to me.

To Dartmoor Prison, The Governor.

The matter of Matthew Faber has been decided. He is to be allowed to escape from custody at midnight tonight. This is an official request. Kindly ensure that it is effected efficiently and punctually.

Mycroft Holmes.

"If this were genuine, I would certainly have been informed," my friend said. "but we will deal with it later. I would be obliged, Mr Crout, if we could repair to Mr Faber's cell now."

The governor nodded and got to his feet. He opened the door and shouted something into the corridor, whereupon a burly guard, different from before, appeared promptly.

"Pickthorne, take these gentlemen to Matthew Faber's cell," he ordered. The guard saluted smartly and led us along the dismal passages, quieter now and echoing with the tread of our boots on the stone floor.

We were admitted and the heavy door closed behind us. The guard had assured us that a single cry would summon him from nearby, in the event of trouble.

Mr Faber lay on his bunk, staring at the ceiling until we entered. At the sight of us he quickly sat up, his cheerfulness giving way to a puzzled expression.

"I had not expected visitors, this evening."

"I am aware of the plan for your escape," Holmes told him. "and I am here to impress upon you - if you venture out, you will be killed shortly afterwards."

"What can you mean?"

"I am attempting to make you understand that you have been the victim of a deception that caused your incarceration here, and will claim your life if we do not speak frankly."

He shook his head. "You speak in riddles, Mr Holmes."

"Then allow me to explain. To begin, let me first give you my solemn word of honour that what I am about to tell you is the absolute truth, and not a means to trap or test you. I am aware that you have been warned against discussing your situation. Mr Ollshaw, I am certain, told you that any such conversation would be such as you implied during our previous visit. In fact, is it not true that all communication regarding this affair was with Mr Ollshaw, and never directly with Mycroft?"

He considered, and suddenly appeared less sure of himself.

"I have not seen or heard from Mr Mycroft since Thomas Ollshaw and I were summoned to his office."

"That is because Mycroft had no hand in the proceedings, other than to have you sent here temporarily at Ollshaw's suggestion. Since then, having misgivings about your guilt, Mycroft requested that I see you and conduct an investigation. This I have now completed."

The prisoner's expression changed. He appeared, to some extent, to have been won over.

"I could not understand why Ollshaw would bring unfounded charges against me," he said then. "He accused me of divulging certain facts to agents of the Kaiser. I swear to you, Mr Holmes, on my life, that there is no truth in this. I am, and always have been, loyal."

"So my enquiries have revealed, you can therefore be sure that you will indeed be leaving this place before long, though not in the way Ollcroft intends. It was suggestive from the beginning that he was responsible for the information making its way to Germany, for if you were innocent who else can it have been? Doubtlessly he was somehow able to gain sight of a confidential dossier or message without the knowledge of Mycroft or yourself."

"But that is impossible!"

"That being the case, it may be that the information was never divulged at all, that Ollshaw somehow arranged with an accomplice in Germany to make it appear so. The end result, to cause you to be imprisoned, would be the same."

"All this time, Mr Holmes, I have believed Mr Ollshaw's assurance that Mr Mycroft colluded with this, with the intention of allowing me to escape to keep an arranged meeting with the Kaiser's agents to whom I was to furnish false information. That is why I was able to remain in good spirits while detained in this place, knowing that my escape was already planned and that, afterwards, I would be returning to London."

"Ollshaw was careful to convince you of that. You would not have survived for long."

Mr Faber looked more perplexed than ever.

"But why? I have known Thomas for years. We were friends. Yet he has come to support the Kaiser?"

"That, as I inferred, has yet to be definitely established. Doubtlessly, Mycroft will attend to it after your reappearance at Whitehall. Ollshaw's reason, for causing your misfortunes at least, concerns your wife."

"Iris?" He was visibly shocked. "How is she concerned in this?"

"Ollshaw wishes to marry her, to replace his dead wife. That is why his scheme was set in motion."

"Does she reciprocate?" He asked in a voice that shook.

"Not at all. Ollshaw has visited her several times since your removal from the capital, but she is unaware of his intentions other than to recognise them as kindness."

"During our interview with her, she spoke only of you and with much concern," I added to reassure him.

"But, if he has received no encouragement, what reason can he have? If he is ready to re-marry, why does he not seek a new wife elsewhere?"

"Because he is not ready to re-marry," Holmes answered. "He remains obsessed with his deceased wife. I believe he looks upon your wife as a replacement, because of a physical resemblance."

Mr Faber's face lit up, as a man's does when an old memory brings realisation.

"I recall an occasion when Mrs Ollshaw identified such a similarity. I could not see it myself, and we laughed about it before it was forgotten as the conversation moved on. It was at a dinner that the four of us attended at Claridges."

"Evidently Mr Ollshaw did not forget, or of he did, it came back to him after his wife's death."

"I could feel sorry for him," Mr Faber admitted, "had he not deliberately endangered my life."

"Ah yes, that is the remaining aspect that must be resolved, before you return to London with Doctor Watson and myself. We will leave you now, but I can assure you with confidence that you will not be a prisoner for much longer."

When this was explained to Mr Crout, he took on an incredulous look. "This is a strange business, and no mistake. What do you intend to do now, Mr Holmes?"

My friend leaned forward in his chair. "From what I have just related, it is apparent that Ollshaw has arranged for some harm to come to Mr Faber, for he cannot allow him to live for long after the arranged 'escape'. It is essential that he dies in order, not only to justify the accusations against him – I imagine the reason that Ollshaw would give to his superiors would be that the traitorous meeting somehow went wrong, perhaps that Mr Faber's intended new masters wanted only information – but to satisfy Ollshaw's desire for Mrs Faber. At this moment Ollshaw knows exactly where to send an assassin, but only until Mr Faber leaves here. I therefore believe that such a person lies in wait not far from the prison, in order to accomplish his work quickly. I suggest that Watson and myself reserve rooms at the Flag and Anchor as before, then return here close to midnight. If you would be so good as to allow two of your men, armed as we are, to accompany us in a search of the immediate area, it may be that we can capture the assassin. Finally I will telegraph Whitehall in the morning, to obtain permission for you to release Mr Faber. Is that agreeable to you?"

The temporary governor sat very still. After a moment he nodded. "On the face of it I can raise no objection. When you return

I will have Pickthorne and another ready with firearms. It is likely that the situation will be complicated," he consulted his pocket-watch, "by the mist that often appears at this hour, so extreme care must be taken."

Less than half an hour later, Holmes and I had taken rooms as before. In the short time available to us we ensured that our weapons were loaded and well oiled, before prevailing upon the innkeeper for a late meal. This the man provided without complaint, and so we were well fortified when we once more entered that dark citadel.

Mr Crout was as good as his word, and Pickthorne and another guard whose name we learned was Renning stood armed and waiting. After a short discussion, Mr Crout wished us well as we departed.

The mist engulfed us at once. Before us lay the moor, in the opposite direction to the small settlement of Princetown.

We reached the coarse earth at the edge of the hidden expanse, finding ourselves in the midst of huge boulders that appeared and then disappeared from our sight in the enveloping cloud. Holmes gave instructions for the two guards to make off in a different direction before we ensured that our quarry was not concealed somewhere around us. We moved cautiously, the strange sounds of the moor disquieting and those of our movements a dull echo. We could hear nothing of the others, indeed it had been thought better not to call to each other for fear of giving away our positions to the waiting killer.

It had begun to enter my head that Holmes reasoning might be at fault, when a sound of a shot from not far ahead preceded a flash of sparks near my face. We became still at once, and I realised that the bullet had struck one of the boulders that towered above us, indistinct in the swirling mist. We listened, but there was nothing.

"I heard running footsteps, further away," Holmes said in a low voice. "I think we should continue slowly, with our ears pricked."

We trudged on in silence, ever wary of each shadow that dimly crossed our path. Once I was startled by the sudden appearance of a tall shape reaching out towards me, but I lowered my revolver as I identified the naked branches of a stunted tree. Holmes put a hand on my arm, and again we were both still. I barely saw that his indistinct form had the alert look of an animal that had scented its prey, as we strained our ears for direction. For a moment there was complete silence, then an owl or some other night-bird gave a shrill cry and I heard the flapping of wings as the creature responded to our disturbance. I felt my nerves release some of their tension, but then the sound of two reports came to us through the fog, accompanied by a scream of terror.

"This way!" Holmes broke into a run, somehow avoiding obstacles that appeared before us, and I followed. We paused once before, hearing faint voices, we hurried on until at last we came upon the two guards standing over the body of a man.

"I got him, sir," Renning said with some relief, "but I swear he nearly did for both of us."

I saw that a double-barrelled shotgun lay on the ground nearby, and reflected that they had indeed narrowly missed death. The assassin had had no chance of survival, for the bullet from Renning's pistol had struck his chest near the heart.

Holmes conducted his observations. "One barrel discharged without finding its target, fortunately, and you fired before the other could be brought into play." He turned to Renning. "You are to be commended."

"I was top marksman in my regiment, sir. Some years ago, now."

"Clearly your skill has not deserted you."

The guards carried the body between them, until we found ourselves in the prison yard. It would now be stored in some convenient place until the local police could be informed of the events of tonight. Holmes mentioned that it would come as no surprise to him to learn that the dead man already featured in their files.

After relating our adventure to Mr Crout we returned to the inn, where we both passed a peaceful night. After an early breakfast I accompanied my friend to the local Post Office which opened for the day as we arrived. He sent the promised telegram to Mycroft, with a shortened account of his discoveries and the subsequent happenings, as well as a request that a message be despatched to the temporary governor to secure Mr Faber's release from custody.

"The unfortunate thing is, Watson," he said as we came to the edge of the moor and took in its vastness under a clear sky, "that we shall probably never know whether Ollshaw's scheme involved the Kaiser's spies or not. It could have been entirely his invention to discredit Mr Faber and have him disposed of before, after some little time had passed, setting out to woo his wife."

"Clearly, the assassin, whoever he was, can throw no light upon that now."

"Or will ever ply his trade again. Renning is an excellent shot. No, the only remaining chance of learning the roots of this matter lies with Ollshaw, but I doubt if he will further incriminate himself unless it is under duress."

I nodded my agreement. "I must confess, Holmes, that I was greatly relieved to leave the moor last night. The atmosphere of the place, and that mist that could have hidden all manner of things, lay heavy on my nerves."

"The memory of the hound, bounding towards us out of the fog still haunts you, I perceive. Take heart, Watson. Those are the ghosts of yesteryear, gone forever and the evil with them. What do you say to a walk along this well-used path, to enjoy such beauty as our surroundings afford until the time for luncheon arrives? From the aromas that emanate from that coffee shop that we passed after leaving the Post Office, I would say that we can expect a reasonable meal there. After that I would think we can return to the prison once again, where a representative of the local force may then be in evidence. Also, by then enough time will surely have elapsed for Mycroft to have given Mr Crout permission to release Mr Faber. Then it is simply a matter of the three of us taking the next train back to the capital, where a very relieved Mrs Faber will doubtlessly be pleased to receive us."

The Adventure of the Doubtful Conviction

Of all the adventures that I have been privileged to share with my friend, the consulting detective Mr Sherlock Holmes, there is one which is always uppermost in my memory from our early days together. His deductions and conclusions I knew, were always founded on inescapable truth, so that the many guilty parties who attempted to trivialise or deny his evidence did so in vain. The official detectives of Scotland Yard, who had once looked upon Holmes' methods with the greatest disapproval, came to understand that his peerless logic was invariably immune to a defence based on lies or false witness. Only once was this brought into question by some who, after some experience of my friend's abilities, had every reason to know better.

I recall gazing from our sitting-room window, one evening in late spring, watching the glow of the sun disappear behind the roofs of the houses opposite our lodgings, when my attention was drawn to a cab as it came to rest below. In the fading light, I recognised the passenger who emerged and strode purposefully to our door.

"We are about to receive a visit from Inspector Lestrade." I told my friend.

Holmes looked out from behind the evening edition of *The Standard* and replied in a voice that betrayed his boredom of recent days:

"Let us hope he brings something of interest. I was beginning to suspect that all of London's criminals had either been incarcerated or decided to retire."

I said nothing, but hoped that his black mood would lighten as we learned the purpose of the Inspector's visit. We heard our landlady answer the summons of the door-bell, and then came the heavy but familiar tread upon the stairs as we waited.

"Come in, Lestrade", Holmes called in response to the knock on our sitting-room door. As our visitor was now so familiar to us, Mrs Hudson had not troubled to accompany or announce him.

The little detective entered and I knew at once that something was amiss. His expression was grave, and his voice cold as he refused Holmes' invitation to sit with us.

"Clearly, something is causing you great concern," my friend observed. "Pray tell us what has occurred."

"Lester Rawe has passed away."

Holmes looked mildly puzzled. "When was this?"

"Two days past."

"In his own bed?"

"In the hovel in Limehouse, where he has lived ever since he came to our attention and probably long before."

"Lestrade, I am aware that Rawe was a burglar of long standing, one of the few who repeatedly foiled all attempts of the Yard's finest to halt his career, but I am at a loss to deduce why you should come here to announce his demise in such an accusatory tone."

The official detective hesitated and I wondered if he regretted his attitude, but when he replied his voice was unaltered.

"On his deathbed, he admitted to entering the house of Miss Annie Kearn, and murdering her."

All was silent for a few moments. Holmes' expression deepened, not unexpectedly, for I was aware of the implications that this news presented.

"That was five years ago," he said. "One Gerald Quince was convicted of the crime and has resided in Newgate ever since. He escaped the hangman because there were doubts about his sanity, and Miss Kearn's set of four antique diamond brooches were never recovered."

"Precisely," Lestrade retorted, "and now Lester Rawe admits - on his deathbed, mark you - that he was her murderer. As I recall, Mr Holmes, it was largely on your evidence that Quince's guilt was established. Your deductions, the smudged footprint, the hair impaled upon the broken window pane, robbed that man of five years of his life. Why, I remember my extreme doubts about your methods at the time, and those of my colleagues at the Yard, but it pleased the court to accept your testimony."

"The conclusion was inescapable. Quince was Miss Kearn's killer. How is it that, after the many times I have aided the Yard since, it takes no more than a doubtful statement by a professional burglar of long standing to bring my methods into question?"

"I hesitate to believe that Rawe would have made a false confession as he faced death. You may recall that he was a profoundly religious man."

Holmes nodded. "A contradictory trait for a criminal, but far from unique. Come, Lestrade, there is more to this, is there not? You would not practically accuse me of negligence on such an insubstantial basis."

"Well, yes," the inspector fiddled with the brim of his hat which he held before him, "there have been questions in the House. My superiors are very displeased."

"Ah, now we get to the root of it. And who may I ask, has been asking such questions, as if I cannot deduce it from reports in the dailies?"

"It was Mr Patrick Ribbert, MP."

"That well-meaning champion of the convicted prisoner. How many robbers and murderers has he sought privileges and sympathy for, during his career of the past two years? The man is deluded, and easily convinced by a smooth-talking solicitor of his client's innocence or remorse."

"Nevertheless, the situation is as I have described. There are still those at the Yard, some far above my level, who have always harboured doubts regarding your procedures. I fear that they cannot be ignored."

Holmes looked up from his contemplatory position suddenly, but spoke calmly.

"What then, do you, or your principals, propose to do?"

"There will be an investigation, of course. The case of Gerald Quince will be reviewed. Doubtlessly some of my superiors will wish to return to other occasions where you have been involved with us."

"That is what I would have expected, in the circumstances. Very well, conduct your enquiries into my methods and even my past behaviour if you must, and I also will conduct my own investigation into the veracity of the confession of Lester Rawe." He rose to his feet. "Now, if there is nothing else, we wish you good evening, Lestrade."

After the inspector's departure Holmes said little, but from his expression I could tell that he was considering the possibilities and probabilities of the problem that had been set before him. Only once did I attempt to intrude upon his chain of thought, remarking that the scant evidence presented stood little chance against his already established reputation.

"That is perhaps true," he replied distantly, "but I will not see this agency brought into disrepute, even in the slightest. If this matter is not corrected there will always be those who doubt our accuracy and integrity, and who knows how many crimes will succeed that I could otherwise have prevented?"

We retired shortly afterwards, with Holmes still in a pensive mood. The following morning I approached our breakfast table to find him already surrounded by papers discarded as he searched his index.

After greetings had been exchanged our landlady entered, and it was after our bacon and eggs were consumed that he enlightened me.

"I have made some progress. It seems that Miss Annie Kearn inherited her brooches, and is known to have allowed sight of them to only one person. The Mayfair jeweller, Saul Brunstein, is reported to have taken charge of them to ascertain whether their aging settings have remained secure. I propose to pay Mr Brunstein a visit this morning. If you have nothing better to do, Watson, perhaps you would care to accompany me?"

"I have a few more days, before it will be necessary to return to my practice. If I can be of any service, I would be delighted."

#

Mr Saul Brunstein's shop proved to be less elaborate than I had expected, and was situated between a milliners and a purveyor of exclusive fragrances in the heart of Mayfair. Our cab having departed, we entered the premises and waited while a young woman selected her engagement ring with her intended looking on. Holmes examined the display cases with some impatience, but I used the brief interval to study the man who was the object of our visit.

Mr Brunstein was tall, though not as tall as Holmes, and had the grey pallor of one who spends little time out of doors. A sombre dark suit was draped around his spare form, and he wore a winged collar and black tie with an enormous knot. I noticed that his body was held slightly bent as he moved, as if from long toil in that position. His age, I estimated, would be about fifty-five years.

Presently, the couple left the shop, appearing delighted with their purchase. Holmes stepped forward instantly to the counter.

"Am I addressing Mr Saul Brunstein?" he asked pleasantly.

At once the proprietor's eyes narrowed.

"You are indeed, sir. How may I assist you?"

"My name is Sherlock Holmes. I am conducting an enquiry at the behest of Scotland Yard concerning a set of antique brooches that I understand you once repaired or examined for their owner, Miss Annie Kearn."

Mr Brunstein did not relax his expression, but replied slowly and carefully after a moment had passed. "I had formed the opinion, Mr Holmes, that you are a private agent who is unconnected with the official force."

"That is certainly the case, although I have aided their investigations to their satisfaction on a number of occasions. The matter I wish to discuss was presented to me by Inspector Lestrade, so I would appreciate your co-operation."

The proprietor paused for an instant, which seemed to be his habit. Then his face adopted a look better described as a grimace, rather than the smile that may have been intended.

"Very well. The brooches were quite unique in my experience, that is why I remember the transaction although it took place five or more years ago. I recall reading that the items were subsequently stolen and the poor lady was killed."

"She was murdered," Holmes confirmed, "but it has now arisen that the man imprisoned for the crime may after all be innocent, since another has confessed. That is the situation from which I am attempting to extract the truth."

Mr Brunstein considered, then nodded slowly.

"There is perhaps a way that I could help. During my conversation with Miss Kearn, she spoke several times of Mr Jake Weller, who was apparently a confidente of hers. I formed the impression that they enjoyed a close relationship, and so he may have information that could be valuable to your enquiry."

"You believe that he may know something of the crime?" I interjected.

"That is doubtful, but he certainly is converscent with both the history of the brooches and the day-to-day life of Miss Kearn. I thought that you might find some sort of direction from him." Mr Brunstein tore a scrap of paper from a pad on the counter, scribbled an address on it and handed it to my friend.

"I am obliged to you, sir," Holmes said. "Can you bring to mind anything more?"

As Mr Brunstein shook his head, I was aware of the door opening behind us. His face lit up as he saw a new customer.

"I regret that I cannot, gentlemen."

"Then we will bid you good morning."

#

Holmes wore a smile of satisfaction as he raised his stick to hail a passing hansom, but after giving the driver our destination we rode in silence.

"Are we returning to Baker Street?" I enquired presently.

He turned to me from observing our changing surroundings. "Try to curb your desire to fill your stomach, Watson. There is, I think, sufficient time to visit Mr Jake Weller before luncheon."

"You are not anticipating that this interview will take long, then?"

"Perhaps not. Are you armed?"

"I have my service revolver," was my surprised answer, "but I had not realised that it would be needed."

"It is likely. I know of Jake Weller. He is a killer for hire. I marvel that he has eluded the attention of Scotland Yard for so long."

"But Mr Brunstein sent us to him." I said incredulously. "Surely he cannot be aware of Weller's history?"

The smile returned to Holmes' face. "I am quite certain that he is. There is little mystery here, I think."

We left Mayfair and Knightsbridge behind and came upon the Kensington Road. The cab came to rest near a short street of terraced dwellings that led off the main thoroughfare. This place was new to me but Holmes seemed to be familiar with it, for he paid our driver without asking further directions. The cab left as we stood on the corner, he glancing from house to house. As we watched, a telegraph boy mounted his bicycle and departed. He passed us by without a glance, but Holmes' gaze was fixed on the house he had just visited.

"As I suspected," he murmured.

"You expected Weller to receive a telegram?"

"I am not surprised to see it, at about this time. How else would Mr Brunstein warn him of our impending arrival?"

"You had misgivings about the jeweller, from the moment you saw him," I concluded, remembering Holmes' demeanour during and after the interview.

"Even before that," he said as we strode towards the house. "Consider the facts as we know them. Miss Kearn was reported to be of a secretive nature, was she not? Who then, knew that she possessed antique brooches of considerable value? I would wager that no one knew, until she entrusted them to Mr Brunner for examination and repair. As he alone knew of their existence, the possibility is that he hired Gerald Quince to steal the brooches, but the crime was discovered. I imagine that Quince hid them in some place as yet undisclosed, and this affair is an attempt to secure his release from prison so that he can recover them."

"But Holmes," I objected, "five years has passed since the robbery and the murder of Miss Kearn. Why would Mr Brunstein, or anyone else, wait for so long?"

"My index indicates that the insanity that has plagued Quince since his incarceration has retreated somewhat of late. It is likely that he was not capable of recollection until now."

We paused, now only yards from our destination.

"So the confession of Lester Rawe was somehow forced?" I ventured.

"Undoubtedly, unless he was a willing conspirator who saw himself as having nothing to lose. Hopefully we will discover all shortly, but now I see that the door is ajar which suggests that our approach has not gone unobserved." He produced his weapon from his pocket. "Stand back, away from the line of fire."

I drew my own firearm, and took up the position that he had recommended. From an oblique angle, he stretched out an arm and pushed open the door fully.

"Mr Weller," he shouted into a room that appeared empty. "We wish to question you about Miss Kearn. There is nothing more against you, as yet."

His words echoed slightly, but were followed by silence. We waited for some minutes, but there was no change or sign of life.

"Very well," Holmes said then, and entered the house.

At once I heard violent movement and my friend slammed the door back on its hinges. A cry of pain was followed by a heavy revolver skidding across the floor, and then a small man in a collarless shirt with a hand pressed against his bruised face was revealed. He staggered towards us but then saw our weapons and stopped abruptly.

"You were lucky, Mister," he growled. 'Another moment and I would have shot you both dead."

"I have no doubt of it," Holmes answered. "I am aware of your reputation, although it is apparently unproven."

"The law isn't smart enough for that."

I saw his eyes flicker towards his lost weapon, which had come to rest a few feet from me.

"I strongly recommend that you abandon all thoughts of retrieving your revolver. Be in no doubt that we will fire instantly, should you make any attempt." Holmes kept his own weapon pointed at Weller's heart. "Watson, be so good as to remove the temptation, and to pick up that telegram form that I see crumpled upon the floor."

I transferred Weller's revolver to my pocket, and opened the screwed-up ball of paper.

Two are coming to you. Be ready. You know what you must do.

I relayed the unsigned contents to Holmes, who nodded.

"How were you intending to dispose of our bodies, Mr Weller?"

"There are ways."

"Of that I am sure, as I am that you have used them before now. Tell me, was it you or Mr Saul Brunstein who induced Lester Rawe to confess to the murder of Miss Kearn?"

Weller scratched his unshaven face, and I saw Holmes' weapon move slightly in response.

"Why should I tell you anything, Mr Sherlock Holmes?"

"Ah," said my friend, "so you recognise me. It would be as well for you to talk to us, I think, unless you are prepared to pay the penalty for attempting to kill us and for whatever means that was used to cause Lester Rawe to falsely confess on his deathbed. That is without mentioning your possible involvement in the robbery and subsequent murder of Miss Kearn. All this you will face alone, for your accomplice will certainly deny his connection. Scotland Yard will, I am sure, be glad to see this crime taken off their books."

Weller stood very still, then seemed to recognise the impossibility of his position. Fear crept into his eyes.

"It's not true!" He cried. "I had nothing to do with that robbery and murder, I swear! I never met the lady, and I didn't know Brunstein in those days. I didn't know Quince either."

"It may be that we, and the official force, can accept your assurance," Holmes said. "But as it is, we would need to have more facts in our possession in order to form an opinion."

"It's like this, see." With the prospect of taking the entire blame, Weller was suddenly eager to talk. "Brunstein knew about the brooches and wanted them. He said they were worth thousands, and the lady didn't fully realise their value. He paid Quince to lift them but it all went wrong. The coppers caught him, but not before he'd hidden the brooches away somewhere. Brunstein went to see him in prison once or twice, but he seemed to be out of his mind and couldn't tell him where the goods were, although he could have been faking it. Once he knew it wasn't the rope for him he might have decided to keep the brooches for himself, if he got out one day."

"So you, together with Brunstein, set about somehow causing the dying Lester Rawe to confess to a murder which he had not committed, in order to get Quince released. After that he would quietly disappear until he divulged, voluntarily or otherwise, the hiding-place of Miss Kearn's property. Is that what was intended?"

"No, not by me!" Weller exclaimed frantically. "It was Brunstein, all of it. I tell you, he's capable of anything. He told me of his earlier life, full of stealing and killings it was, he's not respectable as you might think. It was his idea to threaten Rawe, to tell him his daughter would be found with her throat cut if he didn't confess as he was told. Brunstein hired me to persuade Quince to talk, after we'd got him away, and then to get rid of him."

"I can promise you that Mr Brunstein will receive what is due to him, before long," Holmes assured him. "As for you, your fate will be decided in court. Not that you deserve it, but you may take comfort from the fact that you have escaped the rope yet again, although I think it likely that you will end your life in prison."

Weller scowled, bowed his head and said nothing more.

"Shall I seek a cab for our return or a Post Office, to telegraph the Yard?" I asked Holmes.

"A Post Office, if you would be so good, Watson. I, and my revolver, will keep our friend here company until you get back, and then we will await Lestrade. I am rather looking forward to explaining the truth of this little affair to him, and to hearing him pronounce that my reputation, which was affected as a side-issue, is restored."

The real ending of this affair which, as Holmes described, had little mystery about it, came several months later when both Brunstein and Weller were hanged. Holmes' report to Inspector Lestrade caused the official detective to look into the archives and discover that both men had committed capital crimes in the past, using assumed names.

The antique brooches belonging to Miss Annie Kearn were never recovered.

The Adventure of the Invisible Weapon

From a reference in 'The Musgrave Ritual'.

As I entered our sitting-room one bright autumn morning, I was prepared to find my friend Mr Sherlock Holmes engulfed by one of the black moods that I had come to know well. Declining my company and assistance, he had spent the preceding night with Inspector Lestrade in the capture of the notorious Beecham gang as they attempted to rob the Agricultural and Cattle Farmers Bank by means of a tunnel from a neighbouring shop. Holmes had correctly discerned not only their intentions, but their method and timing of the crime. Consequently, the apprehension of the gang had been effected smoothly by a group of armed constables, and the good inspector had once again added to his formidable record with the approval of my friend.

So it was that I fully expected Holmes to be of a disagreeable state of mind, either as a result of lack of sleep or because no further case had yet presented itself. I saw that he had consumed his breakfast already and that mine stood awaiting me, a steaming plate upon the table.

"I heard you moving about in your room, Watson, and took the liberty of ordering your meal knowing you would present yourself in a few moments. I hope you have no objection."

"None." I reflected that his tone was lighter than I had anticipated, although he had failed to begin with his usual greeting.

The post had evidently arrived, since his eyes had not left the letter he held as he spoke and a small pile of others awaited his attention.

"Interesting," he murmured as he placed the folded sheet aside.

"Did last night's venture proceed well?" I asked him.

His expression lightened. "Exceedingly so. Lestrade was overjoyed, as he has been in pursuit of the gang for a good while. They have eluded him twice within the last six months."

"But no more." I began to eat my bacon and eggs, then: "I recall that you mentioned yesterday that you have no other matters on hand, so may I suggest a bracing walk in the Regent's Park to begin our day?"

"Of course, I had almost forgotten that there remains some days before you return to your practice. Had you made that proposal but a minute or two earlier I would have acquiesced instantly, but I have just read of the problem of Miss Rachel Tarleton of Kirkenfield, near Canterbury. Pray finish your meal and you can then peruse her letter."

I consumed my toast and drank my coffee at a faster rate than I would have otherwise, for I was anxious to see what it was that had captured my friend's interest so quickly. As I pushed my cup away he handed me the sheet of good-quality notepaper that, I had already noticed, was slightly perfumed. I straightened my posture and observed that, for a woman's hand, the script was boldly formed.

Deacon Hall, Kirkenfield.

My Dear Mr Sherlock Holmes,

Please, I need your help desperately. I am going mad with fear.

My father was murdered on his birthday, six months ago, within this house.

My mother was murdered, on her birthday, three months ago, within this house also.

A week from now is my own birthday, so you will see why I am concerned.

I know of no reason for these tragic events, and our local force seem to have made no progress from the first. I apologise for this intrusion but, truly, I have nowhere else to turn.

I have heard much about your remarkable powers so if there is anything you can do, or any advice you can give me that might relieve me of the shadow that hangs over me, then I entreat you to act now, while I still live.

Yours in sincerity and hope,

Miss Rachel Tarleton.

"Well, Watson, what do you make of it?" He had rested his chin on steepled fingers, and his eyes glinted.

"The girl, if she is young enough to be called that, is clearly in a state of panic. If her account is true, that is hardly surprising." I saw in his gaunt features, that he had already decided the matter. "So, I assume you would like me to accompany you to Kent?"

"If you would be so kind, and have nothing better to do."

"I am at your service, of course."

He rose from his chair, his half-empty cup abandoned. "Excellent. Perhaps then, you would care to pack a bag for two or three nights, while I prepare a telegram to inform Miss Tarleton of our impending arrival. I overheard Mrs Hudson speaking to the page earlier, so there should be no delay in its despatch."

Less than an hour later we stood on a busy platform in Victoria Station. Holmes had procured the tickets on arrival.

"I have reserved a compartment in a smoker. It is a short journey, and we should be comfortable."

I heard the train approach and we moved further back as it appeared with billows of smoke and a screech of brakes. When the passengers had alighted there was a great surge towards the coaches by the crowd that surrounded us. We settled into a compartment that smelled faintly of cigar-smoke, the worn leather seats creaking under our weight. The train began to move almost immediately, our surroundings changing from the built-up capital to the leafy suburbs by the time we lit our pipes.

"This sounds like a bad business, Holmes. A curious affair."

He adjusted his thin body to a position where he could more easily see the ever-changing view. "The culprit, of course, is someone close to Miss Tarleton's family."

"Because the murderer is familiar with the birthdays of her and her parents?"

"Precisely. Also, as far as we can tell, it must be someone living in the same house, since there is no mention of intruders. But we shall see."

Little else passed between us during the journey to Canterbury. From there we caught the local train after a wait of no more than fifteen minutes, to arrive at the tiny Kirkenfield Station just before mid-day. A trap awaited us, driven by a cheerful and stout fellow who announced himself rather grandly as Ricketts, formerly coachman and groom serving Mr Godfrey Tarleton and his wife, and now in the service of Miss Rachel.

"Has the purpose of our visit been disclosed to you?" Holmes asked him as we passed the small cluster of shops that surrounded the station.

"Yes sir, yes indeed. There have been terrible things happening at Deacon Hall of late, and now Miss Rachel is in fear of her life as her birthday approaches."

"Your local inspector, I understand, could make nothing of the killings."

"Inspector Willis, between you and me sir, is no longer the man he once was. He is very close to retiring, which is why we were relieved when he requested that Scotland Yard send a man here. Not that much light was shed upon the matter, I'm sorry to say. The fellow was shortly summoned back to London with nothing achieved."

"Do you recall his name?" I enquired.

"He announced himself as Inspector Denning. From the little he said, I gather that he has recently attained that rank, and was sent to us until a more experienced officer becomes available. This we are still expecting."

"Until then, we will see what progress can be made," Holmes said dryly.

By now we had left behind the green lanes and open fields to come upon a wide stony coastal path. The crashing of the sea against the cliff and the squawk of swooping seabirds were clearly audible as our talkative driver turned the trap into a sharp curve, passing weathered animal heads that were no longer recognisable atop tall gate-posts. I saw that sheep were abundant, dotting the distant landscape.

The approach was a short climb, with low-hanging oaks and willows intruding from both sides. Deacon Hall was not as I had imagined it to be, my expectation was of a former manor house or grand residence such as Holmes and I had been summoned to on many past occasions. In fact the building was best described as the remains of a Norman castle, doubtlessly originally intended to act as a seaward watchtower against invading fleets. Some of the battlements and outer quarters were missing, but the tall keep stood solidly before us. Ricketts brought the trap to a halt and unloaded my bag as we alighted, before leading the horse away to be watered. At the same moment the great iron-studded door swung open and an elderly butler appeared briefly, before a young girl in riding clothes strode past him and approached us.

"Mr Holmes," she looked first at my friend, then myself, and back again, "I am so relieved that you answered my call for help. I cannot begin to thank you both."

"That is quite unnecessary," he replied. "Allow me to introduce my friend and colleague Doctor John Watson, whose assistance has been invaluable on many such occasions."

The rush of pride that I felt at his description was quickly replaced by mild amazement as Miss Rachel Tarleton acknowledged me. I saw at once that she was not the frightened, wilting woman that I had imagined on reading her letter, but in her face was strength and determination.

"Welcome to Deacon Hall, gentlemen," she said then. "Pray follow Brookes, who will show you to your rooms, where I am sure you will wish to spend half an hour recovering from your journey. Luncheon will be served immediately after."

She strode away abruptly, leaving Holmes and myself somewhat aghast despite her words of thanks. Brookes proved to be surprisingly sprightly for his age, and guided us to two pleasant rooms that overlooked the sea from the first floor. Within the stated half hour, we assembled in the dining-room that had been apparent to us from the reception chamber earlier. Miss Rachel, still in riding apparel, was already seated at the long table.

I will not go into detail regarding the most pleasant luncheon that we enjoyed. Suffice it to say that Holmes excelled himself in its consumption, though he refused dessert. The conversation was limited to the history of the house, Miss Rachel's response to my enquiry.

"Finally," she concluded, "the original family who had owned the castle since the Norman Conquest became extinct. The man who eventually bought the estate was a churchman, Deacon Berrywell, after whom it was renamed. At his death, during the fourteenth century, my ancestor, Gilbert Tarleton, became the owner and it has been our family home to this day."

Holmes returned his coffee cup to its saucer. "A most interesting and informative account, Miss Rachel, and I thank you for it. Perhaps you would now explain more fully to Watson and myself the circumstances that caused you to summon us here? You have our assurance that we will assist you in any way that we can."

"A moment, and I will explain." She called for Brookes who, accompanied by a kitchen maid who appeared to be approaching middle-age, quickly cleared the table. Wine was brought, but only Miss Rachel partook.

She took a long draught and set down her glass. "I realise that your impression of me from my letter, and from what you must perceive as my lack of grief at the loss of my parents, is likely to meet with your disapproval, gentlemen." She looked to our faces for response and, finding none, continued. "I should perhaps mention that we have never been what might be described as a 'close family', and that we have always produced strong women." She paused. "Nevertheless, I wrote to you with words of truth. For the first time in my life, I confess to being terrified."

"I have already stated that we will do all in our power to put things right," Holmes said with a trace of impatience. "Pray tell us from the beginning of the events here, leaving out not the smallest detail."

She nodded, and spoke quietly after a moment's hesitation. "As I have indicated, we are not a family to be trifled with. Past generations have enjoyed connections to the highest quarters, and many were prominent in their day. My mother once hunted tigers in India, while her sister, Esther, bravely led an expedition across the African continent which, to our great regret, never returned."

"Holmes held up a hand, surprising me as I had expected him to advise her to confine herself to the facts of the case, "Can you recall your age at the time of this venture?"

"My age?" she repeated. "Why, I expect that I was no more than eight years old. Aunt Esther herself had yet to reach her twentieth birthday, but I remember her as a formidable woman. My parents would often argue with her over her allowance, and sometimes concerning the silliest things."

"Thank you. Pray continue when you are ready."

"Ah yes," she said, as if suddenly aware of wandering from the point of discussion, "the murders. Six months ago, Brookes took my father his customary glass of sherry, as he did before luncheon on every birthday, and found him dead in his sitting-room chair. His eyes were wild, as if he had witnessed a horrible and unexpected truth, and it was apparent that he had been stabbed through the heart. Three months later, on the occasion of my mother's birthday, she died in exactly the same circumstances, except that she was engaged in embroidery in the same room."

"When you specify identical circumstances," I said, "are we to understand that the chair was the same, and even the time of day?"

"Excellent, Watson," Holmes murmured.

"That is what I meant," she confirmed. "Except for Brookes' purpose in attending her, which was to bring coffee, the event was repeated. She also was stabbed through the heart as my father had been. The police were summoned at once, on both occasions. Our local inspector seemed baffled and sent to Scotland Yard for assistance, but the officer who arrived was recalled after a short while having reached no conclusions that I know of." At this point, I noticed that a slight tremor had entered her voice for the first time. "You will see then, gentlemen, with my own birthday no more than a week away, why I fear for my life. The murderer of my parents was never seen, nor is his purpose clear."

Holmes' eyes, which had been half-closed as he listened, opened fully and glistened. "You actually saw the bodies of your unfortunate parents, yourself?"

"I did. I am not one to shrink from such things."

"They were both sitting in the same chair, in a similar position?"

"I have said so."

"Did your mother have a fearful expression, as your father did?"

"She looked….confused, as well as terrified."

Holmes nodded thoughtfully. "Pray take us to the room where the deaths took place."

"Certainly." Miss Rachel got to her feet and we did likewise.

We followed her from the dining-room across a corridor to a chamber directly opposite. The sounds emanating from further along the passage, and the aromas, caused me to conclude that the kitchen was situated nearby. Ideal, I recognised, since its close proximity to the dining-room would ensure that food was served promptly with little time to cool.

The sitting-room was large and high-ceilinged, tastefully decorated and dominated by a huge fireplace with several armchairs at either side. A long sideboard, laden with bottles and a water carafe, took up almost the length of one wall.

Miss Rachel indicated the chair in which her parents had spent their last moments, and my friend examined it from every angle, pressing and poking the upholstery here and there.

"Can you remember anything else that was common to both tragedies?" he enquired of her then.

She considered, briefly. "Only the streaks of blood."

Holmes inclined his head. "Pray elaborate."

"There were bloody stripes on the right shoulder of both my father and mother. As if they had been marked for some purpose. That is all."

"One 'stripe', on each?"

"Yes, I am sure of that. Is it significant?"

"It is an example of the necessity of including even the slightest detail, when reconstructing a crime."

"You have said that no sign whatsoever was seen of the murderer," I reminded her.

"That is so, it could have been a ghost."

I saw a quick smile flit across Holmes' face, as I continued.

"Was the weapon ever discovered?"

She shook her head. "Never. That is as much of a mystery as the murders themselves."

"Very well," Holmes said presently. "Miss Rachel, you may leave us to begin our enquiry, if you would be so kind. It would be helpful to interview your butler, Brookes, if he is available."

"You wish to conduct the exchange here in this room?"

"It would be convenient, I think."

"Then I will send him to you."

The elderly retainer joined us shortly and was bade to sit, which he did reluctantly.

"May I ask how long you have served the Tarleton family," Holmes enquired, standing beside me near the fireplace.

"To tell the truth sir, I have quite forgotten. I was little more than a lad when I came to Deacon Hall."

"Quite so. I take it that there is no other manservant."

"That has always been so, sir."

Holmes nodded. "Kindly tell us how many others are employed here at this time."

Brookes reflected. "In recent years their numbers have been reduced. Apart from myself there is the cook, Rowena, Miss Rachel's maid, Kathleen, the kitchen maid, Elizabeth and various outside staff such as the groom, Ricketts and the stable boys." His expression became nostalgic. "We are a small household these days, sir."

"How long has Miss Rachel's maid held her position?"

"Since shortly after Mr Godfrey died. Her predecessor had served here almost as long as I, and retired because of failing eyesight."

"And the cook?"

"Seven years, sir. I recommended her myself, as she is a distant cousin."

"Was that before or after Elizabeth took up her duties?"

"Elizabeth has lived and worked here for five years. A matter of weeks before Ricketts arrived, as I recall."

"Thank you. Pray tell us, have you, yourself, any explanation as to why Mr Godfrey and his wife should have met such a tragic end?"

The butler shook his head. "I cannot imagine. They were the kindest of people and the most considerate of employers. To the best of my knowledge there was no one who wished them ill."

"Is that true also, of Miss Rachel?"

"Most definitely, sir."

I was about to speak, but restrained myself at a gesture from Holmes. He allowed a short silence before his next question.

"It is true, is it not, that the deaths of both Mr and Mrs Tarleton were discovered by you, in this room?"

Brookes appeared suddenly uncomfortable. "It is, sir."

"Then pray cast your mind back. Can you recall anything that struck you as odd, at either time or on both occasions?"

Again, he shook his head. "I do not think so." Then, "Of course, the door. But that was such a small thing."

"Nevertheless, kindly explain."

"It was just that, as I entered the room each time, I found the door ajar. It was unusual for either Mr Godfrey or Mrs Caroline to leave it so."

"As if someone had left the room hurriedly?" I suggested.

"Exactly that, sir"

The remainder of the afternoon was spent interviewing the rest of the staff in their places of work. The stable boys and Kathleen, Miss Rachel's maid, were dismissed quickly since, as Holmes pointed out, they entered service here after Mr Godfrey's death. The cook he reserved for possible later enquiries, together with Ricketts. Finally, Elizabeth the kitchen maid returned from an errand to a local farm to join us in the sitting-room.

"Mr Brookes told me you wished to see me, sir." She said pleasantly.

"That is correct," my friend confirmed. "Please be seated."

When she had settled herself Holmes regarded her with a faint smile. "I understand that you have worked here for some considerable time. Well before Mr Godfrey's death, would you say?"

"Much before that, sir. It must be five years or more, by now."

"Has your time here been to your liking? That is, are you content?"

"Oh yes, sir, as much as a serving girl can be. I have my meals and a roof over my head."

"Quite. Tell us, please, of your situations before coming to Deacon Hall."

She appeared momentarily confused, as if looking back over her life was difficult.

"Well gentlemen," she explained, "I was in a workhouse in Canterbury for most of my early years. When I entered service at Lord Dornington's estate, I was still a slip of a girl. When he passed on I was lucky enough to find a situation here."

"You were fortunate indeed," Holmes remarked, "but can you remember anything from the time of the tragic killings here which might aid our investigation? It looks as if progress will be lamentably slow, but we will stick at it until all is known."

Again she seemed to consider deeply. I concluded that she was probably slow-witted.

"No, sir," she answered eventually, "I can bring nothing to mind. I am sorry."

Holmes shrugged. "It is of little consequence. I am confident that we will shed some light on the events quite soon, regardless." He interrupted to peer at the mantle-shelf near where Elizabeth sat. "What an extraordinary design has been worked into the leather strap of that horse-brass. Pray hand it to me, so that I may examine it."

"Certainly, sir." She rose and complied. Holmes took it from her.

"You may go now, but if anything should occur to you I would be grateful for your assistance."

"Thank you, gentlemen."

She curtsied, and left us.

"What do you make of her, Watson?" my friend asked after the door had closed.

"Elizabeth is no longer young but seems to possess the disposition of a girl. She does not appear to be a quick thinker."

"So it would seem, old fellow. Well, unless I am much mistaken, it is almost time for dinner."

The meal was no less satisfying than that which came before. Again Miss Rachel took the lead in pleasant conversation, replying to Holmes' questions about the neighbouring estates. At its conclusion she gave permission for us to smoke, and we filled our pipes as she finished her glass of an exquisite burgundy that we had already sampled.

"I trust you have not forgotten that Mr Rodney Knox will be with us for luncheon tomorrow," she reminded Brookes as he took away her glass and the empty bottle.

"No, Miss Rachel. I have informed Cook, as you ordered."

As he left I saw Holmes' questioning expression, as she apparently did, since she explained before he spoke.

"Mr Knox is a regular caller, and has been for some time. From his conversation I imagine he will propose to me sooner or later, but I am undecided."

"I am sure that it will be our pleasure to meet this gentleman." I replied.

Shortly afterwards, Holmes asked permission to spend the evening in the library, which was granted. I spent the time in conversation with Miss Rachel, who impressed me greatly as an interesting, if rather excessively forceful, woman. I discovered that the relatives she had mentioned previously were not alone in their memorable experiences. In return, I related some of the adventures in which I had been privileged to accompany, and sometimes assist my friend, in the early days of our association. I was pleased to see that she appeared fascinated.

It was quite late when I left the lady, and I saw that Holmes had already retired. I slept soundly and woke to see sunlight streaming through the curtains. I could hear movements indicating that he had already risen, and so it was no surprise to find both he and our hostess awaiting me at the breakfast table.

"Did you find our library sufficiently entertaining, Mr Holmes?" she enquired when all but the coffee cups had been removed.

"Very much so. In particular, the detailed account of your family history maintained by your late father was most enlightening."

I was surprised to see her expression change to one of incomprehension.

"I knew of no such work." Then she visibly collected herself. "Of course, the affairs of the estate as well as my parents' deaths have prevented me of late from giving my usual attention to our books."

"It would have surprised me, had it been otherwise."

"Have you, as yet, made any progress?"

"I have indeed. In fact I have been able to form four different theories to explain the most regrettable past events here. I can confidently tell you that my enquiries will soon be at an end."

She was about to reply, doubtlessly with a question, when Holmes straightened in his chair and peered towards the window on the opposite side of the room.

"What is it?" I asked him.

Miss Rachel followed his gaze and replied. "If you are concerned about the men you glimpsed from the window, Mr Holmes, I should tell you that they are here quite often. As you know, Deacon Hall is an ancient building. Several times every year, their services are required for minor, and occasionally substantial repairs."

"They must be conversant with the basic structure, then?"

She laughed shortly. "By now, they are more familiar with it than I."

"In which case I must interview them." He rose immediately. "If you will excuse me, Miss Rachel."

With that he left the room, leaving our hostess exchanging a puzzled glance with me. Moments later, we saw him conversing with two workmen who were passing the window. This did not surprise me, for I had long since learned that he could quickly establish a rapport with all classes. Satisfaction was written on his face as he returned.

About two hours later, the promised Mr Rodney Knox arrived.

I had requested that Holmes enlighten me as to several confusing aspects of this affair, and he was about to explain. We stood in the reception chamber, near the sitting-room where the front door was visible to us and we were unlikely to be overheard, when the insistent ringing of the bell brought Brookes at a run. He had the door half-open, when it was roughly pushed the rest of the way. The butler hurriedly stepped aside to allow a tall young man with an arrogant manner to enter, regarding him contemptuously.

"Take these." He forced his hat and stick into Brookes' hands. "Where is she?"

"In the sitting-room I believe, sir."

The visitor strode towards us, looking around.

"Who are you?" he asked impertinently.

"They are visitors, here at my invitation," said Miss Rachel as she descended the stairs.

"I assume there is a good reason for their presence."

"You may assume what you will sir, but as you appear to have forgotten to await the courtesy of formal introductions, I will inform you that I am Mr Sherlock Holmes and this is my associate Doctor John Watson. As for your second question, we are to assist Miss Rachel with some unpleasant difficulties."

"Holmes, did you say? I have heard of your busy-bodying in the capital, before now." He turned to our hostess. "What can you possibly want with these men? Do not pay them a penny, that I must impress upon you. When Scotland Yard decide to send a new man to you, he'll tell you what frauds they are."

An angry outburst, but I noticed that the colour had drained from his face.

I think Holmes would have replied with some force, but before anything else could be said Miss Rachel spoke sternly.

"That is enough, Rodney. If you are here for no other reason than to insult my visitors, you should leave immediately."

"No, I want to talk to you." He gave us another furious look. "In private."

"Very well." She led him into the sitting-room, with an apologetic glance to us that was almost a plea.

"Charming fellow!" I remarked, sarcastically.

"If his intention is to marry Miss Rachel, he will be disappointed. She will already have appraised him and found him much wanting."

Holmes was about to continue our previous conversation, when raised voices from the sitting-room became clearly audible. We both listened in silence.

"I am asking you for no more than a hundred pounds," Mr Knox stated angrily. "I know that you are well able to afford it."

"So that you can gamble away more, in addition to the sum you already owe?" Miss Rachel retorted.

"That is none of your affair."

"Oh, but it is, as long as you are in my debt. It is the extent of my means that is none of *your* affair."

After a moment of silence, Mr Knox appeared to change his tactics.

"Have you given any thought to my question of the last time we met?" His voice had become smooth, even warm, yet I detected an urgent desperation.

"It was unnecessary to do so. As I have already indicated, I am not contemplating marriage to you or anyone else. I have my life here and the estate to run. Really, Rodney, now that my father is gone I can no longer allow you to shoot on my property so there is no reason for any future calls. When you are able to repay your debt, do so by means of my bank manager or solicitor. I do not expect to hear from you otherwise."

There was another silence, longer this time. Then we heard an exclamation of such forceful anger that we feared for Miss Rachel and were about to enter the room, when the door was slammed open and Mr Rodney Knox strode out with frustrated fury written on his face. He passed us without a glance or a word. After snatching his hat and stick from Brookes he left at once, wrenching the door from the butler's hands and closing it with a force that produced a report like a pistol shot.

"Gentlemen, I cannot apologise sufficiently for Mr Knox's behaviour," our hostess said in a subdued tone.

"It is quite unnecessary for you to do so," Holmes replied.

An ironic smile flittered across her lips. "I cannot express regret that we shall not have his company at luncheon."

At that moment, the gong was struck to indicate that it was indeed that time. As we entered the dining-room, I heard faintly a shouting of oaths and the sudden thunder of the hooves of Mr Knox's mount as he took an undignified leave. I pitied the animal, for it was certain to feel the whip undeservedly.

"It would not surprise me," I whispered to Holmes, "if that gentlemen were found to be the cause of Miss Rachel's distress."

"An understandable assumption," he replied. "Until you consider that to create such difficulties would be against his interests. From the exchange that we heard, it seems that Mr Godfrey approved of Mr Knox, even lending him funds and allowing him to shoot grouse or whatever they have here on the estate. Doubtlessly, he was also in favour of marriage between Mr Knox and his daughter, which also suggests that he had a wrong perception of the fellow. To murder him would have done nothing but harm to our disappointed suitor and made the obtaining of further funds difficult, as we have seen."

I did not reply, as Miss Rachel was returning from across the room where she had been instructing Brookes. We rose respectfully as she sat down at the table, her recent embarrassment apparently dispensed with. Shortly afterwards, as a delicious mushroom soup was served, Brookes leaned towards his mistress to speak softly.

"Are the usual arrangements to be observed for the Pagan Parade this evening, Miss Rachel?"

She appeared totally astonished, covering her open mouth with her hand. "Good heavens, with the recent happenings here, I had quite forgotten! Yes, Brookes, we must proceed as we always have. The villagers will expect it, and I have no desire to forget such an old tradition."

"Thank you, Miss Rachel, I will inform the others."

As he retreated she saw our puzzled expressions at once. "A very old ritual hereabouts, gentlemen. I will explain at the conclusion of our meal."

We consumed our roast chicken, gooseberries and cream and coffee with Holmes doubtlessly wondering, as I was, about this new and unexpected turn of events. When Brookes and Elizabeth had done their work and the table was cleared, our hostess related to us what was intended.

"The Pagan Parade, gentlemen, is a very old local tradition," she explained. "Fuel for a large bonfire will by now have been piled high on the common. The folk from miles around usually attend, bringing roasted potatoes, chestnuts and beer. Despite the name, it is not a parade as such, but a frenzied dance by villagers around the flames in ragged costumes. Music is provided by local drummers and flautists."

"These celebrations usually have their origin in historical events," Holmes said then. "Is that the case here?"

"So it is said. According to a 15th century reference in the day-book of our local church, it was an annual happening for the poor to gather and dance after dark on this day. I imagine it was a sort of of premature thanksgiving ritual for the coming harvest. The priest of the time decided that this was worship of the Devil and prohibited any further assembly. As far as I know, there is no truth in this supposition and the parishoners decided to ignore the order."

"That must have resulted in much dispute, in those days," I remarked.

She nodded. "Indeed, but the response was anticipated and easily avoided, by the simple means of changing the appearance of the participants. It became usual for the dancers to be masked, and to wear rags instead of their normal apparel. It is said that even some of the local landowners joined the throng in defiance, for the church was a hard and unyielding influence on the lives of everyone."

"Are we to understand then," Holmes enquired, "that it is your intention to attend the celebration this evening?"

"If I failed to, it would be the first time in centuries that the owner of Deacon Hall was absent. I appeal to you gentlemen to accompany me for I see that you are concerned for my welfare still, although it is not yet my birthday."

"Please bear in mind," I reminded her, "that whoever is responsible for the deaths of your parents, may not adhere to a pattern. Were he to strike earlier, it would be far from the first time that Holmes and I had experienced such cunning."

Resentment flashed in her eyes, as she again demonstrated that she was unaccustomed to argument. I thought that she would certainly attend alone if we failed to comply with her wishes, and I saw in my friend's expression that he realised this too, so it was with no surprise that I heard his response:

"Very well, Miss Rachel. I assume that we will be sitting apart from the other observers."

"Such a tradition has always been maintained. A sort of rough throne is always constructed for the owner of Deacon Hall and companions or family, quite apart from the activity so that a better view of the entire scene is obtained."

"It is against my better judgement, but I see that you will not be moved."

"My thanks to you both. Darkness falls just after dinner at this time of year, so we can set off when we have eaten."

She left us shortly after, and Holmes suggested a walk through the garden in order to benefit from the fresh air. The first autumn chill was already present, but the sky was a cloudless blue and I readily agreed as this struck me as an opportunity to continue my hoped-for explanation of his conclusions.

"If we must attend this fearful charade," he said as we passed beneath an arch laden with wisteria, "we must take care not to let

Miss Rachel out of our sight. To take such a risk is foolishness and I am much against it, but she is that kind of woman who is determined and will not budge from her intentions. We will both be armed, Watson."

"My weapon is ready, as always."

"Stout fellow."

"Will you now enlighten me as to what you have learned so far? There are several aspects of this affair that I find puzzling."

"My case is almost complete, but I lack purpose and proof. However, I have reached certain conclusions that you may wish to hear."

We were well away from the house now, close to a splendid array of colour. Nevertheless, Holmes ascertained that there was no gardener or stable boy in sight before he spoke.

"I will relate to you that which of which I am certain," he began when he was sure that we were quite alone. "For example, what did you understand from the fact that the blood streaks were on the right shoulders of both victims?"

"I…," for a moment I was at a loss for words, then it came to me. "Of course. The murderer is left-handed."

"Bravo, Watson. Now, what purpose do the marks have?"

I considered, but unsuccessfully. "Some sort of signature? A calling-card?"

"Not in this instance. I believe that the murderer simply wiped his weapon free of blood, so that it could be more easily concealed."

"The instrument was never found," I agreed.

"Does it not strike you as strange also, that on *both* occasions the door was left ajar after the killings?"

"It does, but although the murderer fled in that way each time, he was never seen elsewhere in the house."

"Quite so. That is because he did not leave the sitting-room by the door."

"Then how? The chamber has no other exit."

"That is what I asked myself. My conversation with the workmen supplied the answer, earlier."

"Pray enlighten me."

Holmes paused to inhale the fragrance of a late-blooming blossom, before we continued along the path. "We know, by Miss Rachel's assurance, that those fellows are familiar with the design and condition of Deacon Hall. It therefore occurred to me that they might be aware of a forgotten additional entrance. The elder workman mentioned a concealed passage, once used during the Civil War to effect the escape of supporters of King Charles II during a raid by Cromwell's troops. My informant did not know of the sitting-room entrance to this corridor, and was unsure of its continued existence, but he was quite certain of its place of exit."

"Somewhere away from the house. In this garden, perhaps?"

"No, old fellow. The kitchen."

"I would have thought it too small to accommodate a sliding panel, in addition to all the hanging pots, pans and culinary tools adorning its walls."

"You will recall the large recess behind a narrow door, where food and drink are kept cool on occasion by means of marble shelves and the fact that it extends underground. I saw that it was sufficiently spacious to contain a person of normal proportions, if uncomfortably."

I nodded. "Then the murderer waited there until the house was deserted, probably until the early hours, before making his escape?"

"That is a possibility," Holmes answered with a faint smile.

He retired again to the library for the remainder of the afternoon. I imagine that this was to acquaint himself further with the strange local custom of the Pagan Parade. A further stroll among the colourful displays of the garden struck me as a pleasant way to pass the next hour or two, but on returning to my room to regain my pocket-watch which I had accidentally left there I succumbed to temptation and lay atop the bed for a few minutes. I awoke with dinner less than a half hour away, and hurriedly prepared myself.

"Before we embark upon this," Holmes said to Miss Rachel when all but the wine glasses had been cleared away, "there is one thing I must know."

She smiled and put down her glass. "I am at your service, of course."

"Then kindly tell me how many of your staff are to attend with us this evening."

"The answer to that is simple, Mr Holmes. It is customary for two to remain at Deacon Hall during the evening of the Pagan Parade. This is normally achieved by rotation, and this year it is the turn of Brookes and the kitchen maid Elizabeth. The others will make their way to the common on foot to join those in service from other nearby houses, while Ricketts will drive our coach before joining them also."

"Thank you, that is most helpful."

Holmes' expression gave away nothing as he drained his glass.

Later, Miss Rachel, Holmes and I found ourselves upon the common under a full autumn moon. Ricketts had left us to enjoy the company of other coachmen, servants and the like, after ensuring that our conveyance remained at a safe distance near a water trough for the horse.

Already we could see the blaze ahead and hear the crackling of burning sap from the piled branches. Sparks flew up to the darkness above in an unending stream.

The heat became increasingly apparent as we drew nearer, and some of the throng that sat on blankets or various improvised objects cheered and waved as Miss Rachel became visible to them. She returned the gesture as we approached an ancient tall-backed chair that I suspected was kept especially for this purpose, with a rough wooden stool at either side and a gnarled table within arm's reach.

Holmes and I each took a stool and our hostess settled into her place. More cheers erupted from sources now unseen beyond the glare of the flames. A fellow who might have been a local innkeeper laid food and drink before us. At once a rhythmic drumming began, mounting in intensity and accompanied by the frantic tones of several flutes. From the far side of the flames a solitary figure appeared, writhing and spinning in a grotesque parody of dance. Then another appeared beside it, jumping often as if trying to snatch the moon from above. A moment later yet more came into our view, then there were more still in a confused tangle that made counting them an impossibility. The drum-beat grew louder and the movements quicker as the dancers drew close enough for us to discern that the clothing of each hung in tatters and that every face was hidden by a grotesque mask. Some of them cried out, but their words were lost among the music and the roar of the fire. I glanced at my companions, and saw a sort of pride in Miss Rachel's face while Holmes remained expressionless.

Shadows flickered continually across our faces as we ate and drank, Holmes sparingly as was his custom. The scene began to take on the appearance of the tribal rituals that I had witnessed in Afghanistan, and it crossed my mind to wonder at the similarities of the customs of men everywhere.

After a while someone threw a heavy log into the flames and a great shower of sparks obscured out view briefly. The procession before us was momentarily halted by the increased heat until a lone figure emerged. It threw its body about like an acrobat, bending and stretching between somersaults and turning this way and that. I sensed that Holmes had got to his feet at the same instant that Miss Rachel screamed, and I instinctively reached for her and pulled her towards me. Something smashed into the tall chair and I saw that the masked dancer held a pistol. Holmes' return fire was muted by the surrounding noise and his aim obscured by the emergence of the other participants, as the assailant disappeared among them. I steadied Miss Rachel and enquired as to her condition.

"I am unhurt, thank you, Doctor."

"Holmes, were you hit?"

"Not at all, old fellow."

"You see, Mr Holmes, the attack on my life has begun," she said with a tremor in her voice.

"Not so, Miss Rachel. I am quite certain that *I* was the intended victim. Our murderer adheres still to his pattern. We were sitting close together, and Henley is no marksman."

We looked at him in astonishment.

"The stable boy?" I said incredulously.

"How can you tell, in the darkness," Miss Rachel queried nervously.

"Did you not observe that he limped as he fled? During my interview with him I noticed his awkwardness. Nevertheless, I would speculate that his former occupation was that of an acrobat or contortionist, during which he sustained an injury."

"Then it was he who killed my parents?"

"Of that I have gravest of doubts. However, the incident seems to have passed unnoticed, since the procession continues unabated. The glare of the fire will have prevented those beyond it from seeing the attempt. I suggest that we now withdraw without communicating our intentions." His glance settled on me, briefly. "We have some work to do before we retire, Watson."

It surprised me that our hostess offered no resistance. She suggested that we retrieve Ricketts from the crowd that had sat apart from us, now vocally competing with the music, but Holmes would not hear of it. I drove the coach to Deacon Hall, while he conversed inside with Miss Rachel. Ricketts would doubtless find his way home with the others.

There were few lighted windows as we arrived. I saw her into the house before she insisted that I join my friend. Holmes and I led the horse to the stables, where it was given into the care of a young lad who, I learned later, would be there all night in anticipation of the forthcoming birth of a foal. I expected my friend to immediately approach the outdoor staff living quarters, or to lie in wait, but after inspecting the area he gave a sigh of resignation.

"What are we searching for, Holmes?" I asked.

"Henley's body, of course."

"You believe that you fatally wounded him?"

"Not at all. He is, or was, not the murderer. You will recall that he favoured his right hand as he fired."

"Then why did he make the attempt?"

"I suspect that he was somehow compelled. That being so, he could identify the killer and was therefore silenced. In the morning we will inform the local force."

Nor was that the end of the night's events.

We entered Deacon Hall to find no one in sight. Holmes strained his ears to listen, holding up a hand as a signal that I should hesitate also. At first I heard no sound, but his sharp ears led him towards a faint murmuring from the sitting-room. I followed with my hand still resting upon my revolver.

The chamber was lit by candles placed at each end of the mantle-shelf. In their flickering light Brookes and Elizabeth lay as if dead, each sprawled in an armchair. Their appearance was deceptive, since Miss Rachel had already perceived signs of life and was endeavouring to shake Brookes awake.

His red-rimmed eyes flickered open and consciousness returned in a moment, although his expression suggested that he had not recognised us or his surroundings. He mumbled something unintelligible, as his glance took in all three of us, then proceeded to speak in the uncertain tone of one who has committed a grave error.

"Oh, good heavens, I must have fallen asleep. I have never before rested while engaged upon my duties. How can I apologise, Miss Rachel?"

The harsh response that I expected was not forthcoming.

"Apart from this room, have you closed up the house for the night?" She asked him.

"I have, Miss Rachel."

"Then it is time you retired to your room. We will attend to Elizabeth."

Brookes bowed his head in thanks and quickly left us. I turned to Elizabeth, noticing that Holmes was already scrutinizing her and listening to her breathing. I gently pulled up an eyelid and she awoke at once, emerging from her slumber a little more quickly than Brookes, no doubt because of her comparative youth.

"What has occurred, in our absence?" my friend enquired.

She gave us a bewildered look, striving to remember. "Brookes and I each consumed a glass of warm milk in the kitchen, I washed the glasses along with the remainder of the dinner things and we came in here because he wished to show me where the cleaning has proven inadequate. Since then, I can remember nothing, sir."

"Are you feeling ill, now?" I asked her.

"No, Doctor, I am quite recovered." She turned a wavering glance towards Miss Rachel. "I am so sorry. I will see that this does not recur. I beg you not to dismiss me."

"I will consider the matter," our hostess replied. "Now it is best that you sleep, since you will be required early in the morning."

With mumbled thanks, Elizabeth repaired to her quarters.

Holmes regarded Miss Rachel and myself thoughtfully.

"Tomorrow morning I must visit Canterbury," he said. "There I hope to clear up the remaining questions surrounding this affair. I would be grateful if you would allow Ricketts to convey me to the station, Miss Rachel, before summoning a local inspector to search the estate."

"Of course, Mr Holmes. Will Doctor Watson accompany you?"

"I think not." His voice became almost a whisper and his expression grim. "Until my return you must remain in his company at all times. It is not yet your birthday, but the threat to your life has never been greater. Ensure that the door of your bed-chamber is locked, before you sleep."

With that we said goodnight to our hostess, and he spoke to me once more before we parted.

"I am as deadly serious as you have ever seen me, Watson, when I implore you. Do not leave her, even for an instant. Keep your revolver near your hand at all times."

I was surprised to find the dining-room empty next morning. Brookes informed me that Holmes and Ricketts had set off earlier before Miss Rachel appeared a few minutes later. We enjoyed a hearty breakfast, conversing about mundane and unimportant topics, until I brought her down to earth with a reminder of Holmes' warning. I had come to feel that, in order to instil upon herself a state of calm, she had consigned her predicament to the back of her mind, regardless of the attack during the Pagan Parade, but I insisted that she face the situation. The absence of Henley continued, and word had been left at the stables that he must report to her immediately should he reappear, but without result. I used this fact to underline my intention to stay by her side until Holmes' return and, reluctantly because of her forceful nature, she agreed.

The morning was spent riding around the perimeter of the estate. She explained that it was her custom to ensure that the stock fencing was maintained in good order. She was quiet during luncheon, and it seemed to me that her defiant disposition was increasingly at odds with the growing fear that the passing days brought. Sometime later Inspector Willis of the local force arrived to supervise a search of the outbuildings and near area with two constables, in response to Ricketts' visit to Kirkenfield Police Station earlier. They found nothing, and the inspector led his men away with an affronted air at the mention of Holmes' name.

In the early afternoon unexpected visitors arrived. Miss Rachel explained that Mr and Mrs Crowther, an elderly couple, were her nearest neighbours who often came by unannounced to drink tea and discuss local events. When the conversation turned to the Pagan Parade nothing unusual was mentioned and so, I concluded, Holmes had been correct in his supposition that the shootings had gone unnoticed. Several times she gave me a wary look, as if wondering how much to disclose. I shook my head slowly.

The Crowthers' trap had hardly left when Holmes returned in a hired cart. Its driver touched his cap, indicating that my friend had added a generous tip to the fare, and was gone in an instant. Through a leaded window I saw him stride towards Deacon Hall, his expression of satisfaction evident.

"Holmes!" I met him at the door, and we shook hands.

"Has anything further occurred?" he asked at once.

"Nothing," I assured him gladly.

Not long after we sat with Miss Rachel in the sitting-room, the door locked and our coffee cups emptied.

"Well Mr Holmes," she began. "Doctor Watson and I have anticipated your return anxiously. I trust your efforts have been rewarded."

She was feigning a brave face I thought, but the fear in her voice was unmistakable.

My friend leaned forward in his chair. "They have indeed, Miss Rachel. I see that there are almost two hours separating us from one of your excellent dinners, so we have ample time to conclude this case and remove your anxieties. Watson has explained that your local inspector has found nothing amiss here as I expected, but no matter. While in Canterbury I took the precaution of telegraphing Scotland Yard, and a response should be soon forthcoming."

"Thank you," she said. "Any further assistance is most welcome. Please continue."

"Very well." I wondered if she read his expression, as I did. "As I have already confided to Watson, the first thing that struck me as strange was that the sitting-room door was left ajar in both instances, and I was able to establish that this was to give the false impression that the murderer had left the room in this way. The exit was actually accomplished by means of a concealed passage which connects with the kitchen. I considered at first that the cool room there was used as a hiding place until conditions were right for escape, but as there is no outside access I was forced to the conclusion that the murderer *works there*. Now we come to the bloody streaks on the right side of both bodies." He paused and adopted a more gentle tone. "Forgive me, Miss Rachel, for my lack of sensitivity here."

She said nothing, but shook her head to indicate that he should not spare her feelings. After a moment, he resumed.

"Those marks were neither a signature nor a signal. They were left by the wiping of the weapon to clean the blade so that it could be hidden in plain sight, but they indicate that the killer is left-handed. By observation and various simple tests, I have ascertained that two people only, beside yourself, are so disposed. They are the kitchen maid Elizabeth, and your personal maid who we see so little of, Kathleen."

Our hostess sat up straight, her eyes bright. "But Kathleen was employed here since the death of my father, so his murderer was...."

"The woman you know as Elizabeth," Holmes finished.

"But for what purpose?" I asked my friend.

"That will become clear in a moment. I fear, Miss Rachel, that my enquiries have revealed further facts that may shock you."

She collected herself with difficulty. "Kindly proceed, nevertheless."

"One of my calls in Canterbury was to the office of Mr Sinclair Lomax who, as you have mentioned to me, is now the head of the firm of solicitors who have been concerned with the affairs of your family for years. He is, as you know, quite elderly and, when I had explained that I represent your interests, was willing to disclose to me a portion of your family history. You will recall relating to

Watson and myself the doings of your Aunt Esther, who as a young woman led an expedition to Africa." She showed surprise, but he did not wait for her reply before continuing. "It seems that you failed to tell us, probably because you were unaware, that the expedition was financed with money stolen from her father, your grandfather, Mr William Burnside. Esther Burnside had taken up with a certain Byron Jacques, known locally as a notorious thief and kidnapper, and at his instigation and because the police were closing in, stole the money and fled with him abroad. Jacques is said to have been bitten by a cobra and died in the Transvaal, but your aunt eventually returned to England."

Miss Rachel looked at him coldly. "Mr Holmes, are you saying that my kitchen maid is in truth my aunt who I believed to be long dead?"

"I regret that the conclusion is inescapable. Her resemblance to yourself is thinly disguised but there, once you are aware of it. All of her history that she presented is fictitious. The Canterbury workhouse where she claims to have been brought up perished in a fire, years ago, and no one in the late Lord Dornington's employ has any knowledge of her existence. She arrived here five years ago with forged references which, for some reason, were not checked."

"My father tended to take too much on trust. I often warned him of the dangers."

"The significance of birthdays is now also apparent. It was on Esther's nineteenth birthday that she left her family home under a cloud. For that reason she considered it in some way appropriate that every step taken towards gaining mastery of Deacon Hall should be on the birthday of the victim."

Our hostess fixed her eyes on the carpet, her expression one of gloomy disbelief. "This cannot be," she murmured repeatedly.

"What of Henley?" I asked Holmes.

"According to one of the stable boys who I questioned early this morning, Henley confided that he was being blackmailed by Elizabeth. Apparently there was some trouble with a married lady in Kirkenfield, and the resulting scandal would certainly have meant his dismissal."

Miss Rachel stood up suddenly. "Excuse me, gentlemen."

She strode to the door, unlocked it and called for Brookes. Moments later she resumed her seat and spoke quietly, grim-faced. "Now we will get to the end of this. I have summoned Elizabeth."

The woman, who I now realised appeared much younger than her true age, entered and stood before us, seemingly puzzled as to who to address.

"Mr Holmes wishes to question you, Elizabeth," Miss Rachel said in a strangely calm voice.

The kitchen maid turned her innocent gaze on Holmes and myself. "Yes sir, what is it that you wish to know?"

"You will recall that I explained the purpose of my enquiries to you previously," my friend began.

"Of course."

"I have now completed those enquiries to the extent that but one question remains, and none but yourself can provide the answer."

She took this impassively, but when she spoke I fancied that wariness had entered her voice. "But whatever could that be?"

"Simply tell us where you have hidden the body of Henley, the stable boy."

Her expression remained unaltered, so that for an instant I believed that Holmes had made a terrible mistake. His eyes were locked on hers in an unflinching stare.

"I do not understand, sir. How would I know such a thing?" But she was moving, slowly and deliberately, towards the sideboard that held the drinks tray.

"Watson!" Holmes exclaimed sharply.

The kitchen maid ran to seize the water carafe and withdrew the glass stopper so that it seemed she was about to drink without permission. Then I saw that a long and cruel-looking blade was attached and realised that Holmes had warned me against the weapon that had killed twice before in this room. But now its hiding place was revealed – hardened, transparent glass is perfectly hidden when submerged in water. I assumed it had been replaced recently in preparation for Miss Rachel's birthday, as to have let it remain in the carafe since the last murder would have invited discovery.

"If you fail to drop that knife immediately, I will fire without further warning," I assured her.

Her eyes met mine, and I fancied I saw a trace of madness there. She took a pace towards me and I raised my revolver to point at her heart. She saw the resolve in my expression, and shifted her gaze to Holmes, and finally to Miss Rachel. Hopelessness crept into her face, and the knife fell to the carpet.

"How did you know of the blade?" she asked Holmes as he secured her hands with police handcuffs.

"I interviewed the merchant who made it for you, not three hours ago in Canterbury. He was the fourth tradesman I approached. Apparently the fellow was confused as to your purpose in requiring it. The reason you gave him was unconvincing."

When she was seated I stood guard over her, returning to Holmes' previous question. "It is all up with you now, it can be to no advantage to keep poor Henley's whereabouts secret."

She stared into my face with an eerie calmness, looking quite different. It seemed that some of her youthfulness had fallen away, revealing a face much fashioned by years of wrongdoing and a nature turned always towards self.

"Very well," she said in a voice quite unlike that she had used until now. "He lies in a shallow grave quite close, near the edge of the forest to the east of the estate. I had prepared his resting place before I caused him to attempt to rid me of you at the Pagan Parade. You will have realised that I gave opium to Brookes to ensure that he would be unaware of my absence when I left to dispose of Henley afterwards."

Holmes nodded. "I saw that there was a marked difference between his condition and yours, on awakening. Watson later confirmed this."

At that instant Miss Rachel rose and strode across the room to confront the prisoner. Her face had darkened with rage, and I sensed that she was exercising great restraint.

"Are you truly Esther Burnside?"

The kitchen maid looked up, unruffled. "Can you not see it?"

"And you are the murderer of my parents?"

"They were obstacles, a barrier to my rightful life."

"What do you mean? You chose to spend your life as an adventurer, having no connection with us."

"When I took the money to enable my escape with Byron, I discovered that my father had, for reasons of his own, settled a great deal of money upon yours. I returned to England alone and destitute, to find you living as I should be had that money been my inheritance. I entered your house, hoping that my credentials would not be closely scrutinized, and waited. The time came when the urge to regain my rightful place became too strong to delay my actions further. It was time to begin my reappearance by removing those who would have prevented it, one by one."

"So, you intended to claim Deacon Hall on some future occasion?" I speculated. "How was your sudden reappearance to be explained?"

An artful and remorseless glint appeared in her eyes. "I was to leave as Elizabeth and return after an appropriate interval as myself, having recently arrived from Africa and read in the newspapers that Deacon Hall now had no claimant. I can prove my lineage. I would have had little difficulty, for to change one's appearance somewhat is a simple matter."

"You have murdered my parents," Miss Rachel repeated in a voice that hardly contained her anger, "and others. Also, I cannot see the end to the shame you have inflicted upon our family. You would be an outcast for the remainder of your life, were it not that the hangman will take you. God knows," the strength of her family's womenfolk filled her voice, "that I would like nothing better than to undertake the task myself."

I believe that Holmes was about to retort that the law would act sufficiently, and that our hostess should do nothing more than set her mind on her recovery from the dreadful events of the last few months, but his whispered words were cut short as Brookes entered the room with a tall man, indistinct in the shadows of the corridor, standing a few feet behind him.

"Our expected visitor, Miss Rachel," he announced. "Inspector Gregson of Scotland Yard."

Miss Rachel continued to maintain a malevolent stare at our prisoner as if she had failed to hear, but Holmes and I turned to see the official detective enter.

"Ah, Gregson," my friend said with surprising lightness. "Do come in. We have just heard an extraordinary story that will prove your case, and will doubtless do wonders for your reputation."

The Adventure of the Substitute Murder

The investigations with which I was privileged to assist my friend, the consulting detective Mr Sherlock Holmes, were of a wide and varied nature. Not only were his clients from all levels of society, but their problems or complaints differed significantly. Time also was never a constant factor. At the commencement of each case we were plunged into a mystery that would require ten days or ten weeks, or less, before light could be shed where there was darkness before. Many examples of his brilliant reasoning I have recorded elsewhere, but in reviewing the contents of my despatch box I have rediscovered my account of a short incident that I have so far neglected to share with those students of my friend's methods who may have some interest in the matter.

"Mr Sherlock Holmes, sir?" enquired the shabbily-dressed man who Mrs Hudson had shown into our sitting-room.

"I am he," my friend confirmed.

"I wonder if I might take up a little of your time, sir?"

"Presumably you have reason to require my services?"

"Oh yes, yes indeed, sir. Is it true that you sometimes take on cases without charging a fee? I mean, if they are peculiar enough to interest you?"

Holmes and I exchanged a quick glance. It did not surprise me that our visitor had asked such a question, for his appearance was somewhat worn and bedraggled. His hat and coat, which I had just relieved him of, were of the fashion of several years ago, and his face bore the growth of two or three day's beard. I would have said that he was past his fortieth year and, from the faint smell of whisky that surrounded him, a regular patron of one or more of the capital's taverns.

"My fees are charged on a sliding scale, but it is true that they are waived in certain circumstances. However, it will cost you nothing to tell us of whatever has brought you here. I have no engagements until the end of the week."

"If you will come this way." I guided our visitor to the basket chair, near to the roaring fire that our landlady had lit for us against the January cold.

When we were all three seated Holmes asked our visitor if he would like tea. He declined, I thought in the hope that he might receive a stronger beverage, but my friend had evidently decided that the man had drunk enough.

"Very well, then. If you will kindly inform us as to what has aroused your curiosity enough to seek the advice of a consulting detective, we will endeavour to assist you. I assure you that Doctor Watson," he indicated me with a gesture, "is the soul of discretion. He has been instrumental in solving some of my most baffling cases."

As always, I felt a rush of pride when my friend paid me such compliments.

Our new client nodded.

"Glad to make your acquaintance, Doctor."

"And I yours, sir." I replied rather doubtfully.

"Pray commence your narrative," Holmes said with a trace of impatience.

"Yes, of course sir." Our client shifted in his chair rather nervously. "My name is Abram Stirk, I am a cobbler by trade, living with my wife in Putney."

He paused, perhaps to gather his thoughts, and Holmes remarked:

"I had already deduced your occupation. The marks between your thumb and forefinger from encompassing the last as you trim the leather to fit the boot is unmistakeable."

"You are a wizard, sir. I swear I have met none like you, before now."

"It is a simple matter of observation. But please, forgive my interruption and continue."

"The fact is, sirs, that I am beginning to wonder if I was seeing things, if I shouldn't have bothered you after all."

"It can do no harm to tell us, regardless."

"I suppose not. Well, it happened yesterday afternoon. My wife told me she had a mind to make a nice apple tart, to eat after the beef stew that was bubbling away in the kitchen, and I thought that sounded good. I went out into the little piece of land that we call our garden, and realised that the only apples left on the tree were very nearly at the top. I borrowed a ladder from a neighbour and set it against the trunk and climbed as far as I could to fill the basket I had taken with me. When I realised that the winter had spoiled the few that were left, I chanced to look across to the house of the people next door. They have lived there for about two years. We know them by sight and to pass the time of day with but not well, you understand, but there they were. I very nearly dropped the basket, I can tell you. Mr Lester Baggott and Esther, his wife who is known and avoided because of her foul-mouthed exclamations, stood in the room that I imagine is their bedroom. I saw them, clear as day."

Mr Stirk ceased to speak then, and looked at us as if his words should have some significance. Holmes now had a glint in his eyes, and I wondered what I had missed.

"You are quite certain of this?" my friend enquired. "You could not have been mistaken?"

"I have seen him many times before, sir."

"Yes, but on occasion a trick of the light, the reflection through a window…"

"I was so surprised, that I stood there on the ladder, basket in hand, for a good while until I got a better look. It was him, all right."

"Then you had reason indeed to consult me. But tell me, pray, why did you not approach the official force? Inspector Lestrade would doubtlessly have been as surprised as yourself, on hearing such news."

Our client fixed his eyes on the carpet for a few moments, appearing ashamed.

"I am well acquainted with Inspector Lestrade, and Inspector Gregson and others. I have a history, you see, of visiting Scotland Yard on charges of drunkeness, and of petty theft. I did a short stretch once, it's true, but never since have I stepped off the straight and narrow. This I swear."

He paused again, and I seized the opportunity to interrupt.

"Holmes, I know nothing of this. Who is this man Baggott?"

"He was, or is apparently, the sole remaining perpetrator of the Agricultural and Domestic Breeders Bank robbery of about six weeks ago. Two bank employees were killed during the procedure along with, thanks to the fortunate close proximity of the official force at the time, all the robbers except Baggott. Two weeks later he is known to have met with an unknown man in a derelict house in Wandsworth, it is thought to be about arranging an escape route, but fire broke out and quickly consumed the place. The remains of the single body that was recovered were identified as those of Baggott. If I recall correctly, enough of his clothes and the medallion that he wore about his neck were sufficient to satisfy the examining authorities. No trace was found of the other man."

Briefly, silence descended upon us. The shouts of an unknown trader, selling his wares as he progressed along Baker Street came to me faintly through the closed window, and I was aware of the familiar sounds of our landlady's movements below.

A thought then occurred to me that Holmes seemed to have overlooked.

"Could it not have been a close relative of Baggott who resembles him, that you saw?" I asked Mr Stirk.

"No, Doctor. I am certain it was he."

"Baggott has no relatives," Holmes explained.

"To think," Mr Stirk continued, "that we lived close to him without suspecting his true nature. We believed him to be a tanner."

"It is more common than one would think for a person in an acceptable profession to, in actuality, be living quite a different life." Holmes observed.

Our client leaned forward in his chair, eagerly.

"But will you take the case, Mr Holmes?"

My friend considered for a brief moment. "Clearly this man must not be allowed to escape, if it is possible to prevent it. You may leave the sharing of this development with Scotland Yard to us, Mr Stirk, and I will begin my own investigation immediately. My thanks to you for bringing the situation to our attention and now, if you will leave your whereabouts and any other relevant details with Doctor Watson, I will bid you good-day. Be assured that you will hear from us soon."

With that we all three rose, and I took up my notebook to record our client's information to his dictation. Holmes gazed from the window moodily, hardly acknowledging Mr Stirk's thanks and departure minutes later.

"I take it that we are bound for Scotland Yard?" I enquired when we were once more alone.

Holmes consulted his pocket-watch. "It is almost time for luncheon. After that, if you would care to accompany me, I think a visit to Wandsworth might be enlightening."

Of late I had suffered some digestive problems, but the preparation that I employed since had proved effective. It was with considerable appreciation therefore, that I consumed Mrs Hudson's curried fowl. That Holmes did not share my enjoyment came as no surprise. Having eaten little, he pushed the remainder of his food around his plate while exhibiting, to my experienced eye, his usual signs of impatience to begin a new enquiry. Indeed, I had hardly finished my dessert when he rose quickly from the table to put on his hat and coat. As I followed his example, he stood with his head tilted to one side.

"I hear a hansom slowing near our front door, Watson. We may be about to acquire another new client. Otherwise, if we hurry, it may prove to be the conveyance that will deposit us at the derelict house where Baggott was thought to have perished."

We descended the stairs at a fast pace, in time to hail the hansom before it could proceed.

"Twenty-three, Old Albion Street," Holmes instructed the cabby, who shook the reins to encourage his horse to set off at a fast trot.

It was not difficult to see why Baggott and the unknown man had chosen this Wandsworth Street for their clandestine meeting. Number twenty-three was part of a line of ruined structures, but unique in its charred and collapsed interior.

"What is it that you hope to find here, Holmes?" I enquired as we stepped from the uneven pavement into the blackened shell.

"Evidence of what truly occurred."

Beams that were now little more than charcoal and metal fittings blanched by heat crunched beneath our boots as we wandered across a space that had once contained separate rooms. Several times, Holmes picked up large wooden fragments which he immediately discarded. Presently, he stood still in the centre of the debris and looked above us at the featureless grey sky.

"This is where the upper stories would have fallen," he murmured.

He retrieved another charred ember, and his purpose came to me suddenly. The fragment he held had a discoloured handle attached to it. He was inspecting the remains of the internal doors! He discarded it and plucked another that appeared similar from the wet and blackened mass, twice more before his expression changed instantly. He held the ember high, so that he could peer into the lock cavity.

"What have you found?" I asked him.

"Exactly what I expected to find."

He held it out to me. "Do you see?"

"The keyhole is blocked."

"Precisely. You will recall that the account in *The Evening News* mentioned that a key was discovered not far from the corpse.

It was assumed that the body was that of Baggott because of the remains of the clothes and the medallion, and that he had hidden himself here only to fall asleep inside a locked room when the fire started. It was further assumed that the cause was a discarded cigar or cigarette from him or a candle accidentally knocked over."

"That was the official interpretation, as I recall."

"Yet our client claims to have seen Baggott alive and well. The obvious conclusion, if he is correct, is that Baggott killed or rendered unconscious whoever was with him and substituted the body so that it would be taken for his own."

"Could it be that he feared his victim might awaken and somehow force the mechanism before the smoke could overcome him, after he had left the scene himself?"

Holmes nodded. "Possibly, if he had taken the key with him. Hence, as you have just observed, a wooden peg has been driven into the lock."

"You believe then, that the meeting was arranged with the secondary intention being to give the impression that Baggott had perished?"

"I am quite convinced of it. When it is considered that it was he who planned the bank robbery, it seems most likely that he would have allowed for his escape in some way. No one seeks a dead man. We have no way of knowing whether the victim first supplied Baggott with the expected information to aid his disappearance."

I looked again at the ruined interior. "Have you deduced anything further?"

"Only that our client's statement, that he actually saw Baggott since the man's supposed death, is most likely true. I wished to satisfy myself that his observation was not as a result of his excessive alcohol consumption. You will recall that his scent was not unlike that of a brewery-man's apron."

"Indeed," I recollected with distaste.

My friend spent a few moments poking the ashes with his stick, before deciding abruptly: "I cannot see that there is anything more to be learned here, Watson, so we may as well return to Baker Street."

We walked through several streets of that dilapidated district before we encountered a hansom that had just delivered a fare nearby. Mrs Hudson served a delicious steak and ale pie soon after our arrival but Holmes, unlike myself, still had little interest in food. I saw that his mind still dwelt on the case and attempted, correctly for once, to anticipate his next intention.

"We are for Scotland Yard, I presume, in the morning?"

He nodded. "When you have finished somewhat excessively feeding yourself at breakfast, Watson."

The evening passed without incident and, as it happened, our first meal of the day was over quickly.

Soon after, I raised my stick to a passing hansom as we left our lodgings.

"It will be interesting to see Lestrade's face," Holmes said as we neared our destination, "when he learns that Baggott still lives."

We were soon to witness the inspector's response.

"Are you quite sure of this, Mr Holmes?" His bulldog-like face was full of incredulity.

"I have confirmed my client's assertion. The remaining participant in the Agricultural & Domestic Breeders Bank robbery did not perish in the Wandsworth fire."

"I had my men scour the building, while it was still hot."

"Of that I have no doubt, Inspector, but they began with the assumption that the body they discovered was that of Baggott since they knew of no other presence at the time. After my client's revelation and my examination of the house I knew that Baggott had left indications to that effect, to deliberately confuse any remaining pursuit. I cannot imagine the reverse – why would the other man leave Baggott to the mercy of the flames, when he had been hired by him to effect his escape?"

"We now have our suspicions, as to the identity of the other fellow."

Holmes raised his eyebrows. "Pray enlighten us."

"A money lender, who we believe ran a profitable side-line in arranged passages for those who wish to escape the law, has not been since the Wandsworth incident. His name is, or was, Leo Golder."

"Such people do not provide goods or services until they have received recompense in advance," I remarked. "Was the remains of any payment discovered among the wreckage?"

Lestrade shook his head. "None."

"Probably, Baggott secured the information required for his escape by trickery or threats," Holmes suggested. "It would then be unnecessary for money to change hands, and Mister Golder's body could be used to encourage the conclusion that Baggott had met his end."

"Not one penny of the stolen money has ever come to light."

The inspector said it rather sadly, as if he considered this a personal failure. A few moments of silence passed between us, then we heard the heavy tread of boots in the corridor and someone issuing stern orders.

Holmes rose and I followed.

"Well, Lestrade," my friend said, "It may be that we can improve upon the situation. Also, with every constable on the beat watching for him, Baggott will find his departure from the capital far more difficult. We will of course keep you advised of any progress in our investigation."

"Thank you, Mr Holmes. Good day, gentlemen." But Lestrade too, would be alert for any sign of this man whom the Yard had thought to have passed from this world, or for the money of which there had been no sign. It was in his voice, and his expression.

We had been, I estimated, on our way back to Baker Street for fifteen minutes when Holmes half-rose from his seat and called to the cabby.

"Driver, stop here if you please."

"We have not yet reached Baker Street, sir."

"No, but we need to alight. I have just remembered an appointment."

"Very good, sir."

Our conveyance came to a halt and we climbed out. I noticed that Holmes paid the full fare, and the cabby touched his cap in appreciation.

"Why did we leave the hansom?" I enquired. "Must you walk with this cold wind in our faces, in order to think?"

A quick smile passed over his hawk-like features, and he drew me into a doorway. "Not at all, Watson. I noticed the landau that is still following, making consistent and identical turns to our hansom since we left Scotland Yard. I very much fear that Mr Abram Stirk may have met with some harm."

I regarded him curiously. "How can you know that?"

"Because the passenger in the landau knows of our involvement. I believe that Baggott or an agent of his followed our client when he came to consult me, and it seems likely that afterwards he intercepted Mister Stirk, who was apparently noticed when he originally saw Baggott, and questioned him forcibly. Anyone who knows that Baggott still lives is in mortal danger."

We remained in concealment until the landau had passed and was out of sight. Holmes then procured another hansom which took us to the nearest Post Office and then back to our lodgings. At Holmes' direction, the cabby left us a short distance from our front door. We stood silently in a narrow alley for fully ten minutes, before he observed:

"As I suspected. Our lodgings are being watched."

"So now we must devise a way to enter unobserved."

"Much to the contrary, it will suit our purpose well if they see us."

I glanced at him, and he smiled at my puzzlement.

"We must remain in our rooms," he explained, "until the replies to the telegrams which I have just despatched are forthcoming. Also, it will be as well if the attention of Baggott, if it is him, is concentrated here for the time being."

As we strode openly down Baker Street and entered our lodgings I was still unsure of Holmes' intentions, but I have long since become accustomed to that situation.

Mrs Hudson appeared soon, with our luncheon of turkey and ham pie. Holmes ate mechanically, often rising from the table to look out from the window at an oblique angle. As I pushed away my plate I heard the door-bell ring, announcing the arrival of the telegraph boy.

"As I supposed," Holmes said after tearing open the envelopes, "Mr Stirk was assaulted and threatened. Fortunately he was not badly hurt, thanks to the intervention of a constable on the beat. He disclosed our participation in this affair first, regrettably. Later he was taken to the local infirmary. The telegram was from his wife."

"And the other message?" I enquired.

"From Barker, the private enquiry agent that I have used on occasion."

"He is to join us in capturing Baggott?"

"No, he is to delay him, allowing us to leave here unmolested."

I nodded. "So that we will not be observed. Baggott will believe that we are still in our rooms."

"Not at all. I *want* him to see us leave, because I would not put it past such an unscrupulous fellow to plant explosives here during the night, or to waylay Mrs Hudson for knowledge of us. When Barker desists, soon after we leave, we will have a head start but Baggott will again follow until we elude him. All that is required is that he is made aware that we have left these premises. I have made arrangements for Mister Stirk's protection until Baggott is apprehended and, as we are the only others who know that he still lives as far as he can tell, we can expect his continued attention."

About fifteen minutes passed, during which, if I positioned myself as Holmes had done, I could see the landau waiting further along Baker Street. Apart from normal traffic of vehicles and pedestrians there seemed to be no movement until, to my surprise and my friend's amusement, a surly crowd of roughs appeared suddenly and came to a halt. There appeared to be a dispute in progress, since several of them began to shout loudly and push each other aggressively. As we watched blows were exchanged and the crowd was thickened by passers-by and, I noticed, this display had spread to the extent that the landau's movement was completely blocked. The horses must have witnessed similar events before now, since they did not appear disturbed, but the coachman immediately began to berate the brawlers and threaten them with his whip.

"I really must commend Barker," Holmes remarked. "Take up your hat and coat, Watson, for I see that a hansom has approached from the opposite direction and is about to be paid off. If we hurry, we will be its next passengers."

The cabby was evidently known to Holmes, and possibly had been in a similar situation with him before, since a few exchanged words brought a smile to his face and he set his horse off at a fair speed before we had settled ourselves in our seats. I glanced back, to see the driver of the landau furiously increasing his efforts to clear his way ahead.

"If they get too close, our driver has some skill at proving elusive," Holmes assured me. Because of a profusion of drays and other heavy traffic, the landau appeared but once and a long way back. When it was out of sight once more our driver turned his vehicle into a network of narrow alleys, and on emerging we were quite alone in a quiet street. From then on the route to Limehouse held no difficulties for us.

With the journey over and the cabby paid off, Holmes led me into a busy thoroughfare. The houses here were soot-blackened and in need of repair, and residents of various nationalities glanced at us suspiciously. Scantily-clothed children sat on doorsteps and on the pavement, eating or watching. The smell of the place was appalling.

My friend produced a key as we approached an anonymous door between a public house and what looked to me like an opium den.

"I must apologise for not preparing you adequately for our temporary surroundings," he said as the door opened and I was ushered inside. "This is one of the little retreats that I keep around London that have proved invaluable on many occasions. It is not in the most pleasant district I grant you, but I do not expect that we will be here for long."

The house had a sitting-room, a kitchen and a single upstairs bedroom, and was much tidier and cleaner that its outside appearance suggested. He showed me the contents of the huge old-fashioned wardrobe, which were the clothes and uniforms of many professions, and those of the chest of drawers which contained theatrical make-up and items of false hair. After we had refreshed ourselves with cups of strong coffee, he announced that it was necessary for him to go out for a while.

"Just to the docks, Watson. If our friend Mister Baggott intends to leave our shores for the Americas, as I suspect, it will be as well to know the time of his planned departure. I may send a message to Lestrade also, in order to prevent it. There is more coffee in the pot if you so desire, and I have brought along the early edition of *The Standard,* in order that your mind will be occupied."

With that, he repaired to the upstairs room, to emerge in a short while with the appearance of a surly dock-worker who bore absolutely no resemblance to his usual self.

"I do not expect to be long," he said as he left. I heard the front door slam, a few seconds later.

He returned before much more than an hour had passed. I abandoned my newspaper as he shouted a quick greeting and took to the stairs. In a remarkably short time he joined me, having regained his normal appearance.

"Were you successful?" I enquired as he took a seat before the tiny fireplace that I had set ablaze.

He took out his old briar and lit it. "I was, eventually. By the time I had reached the fourth shipping office with vessels sailing for the United States within the next few days, I was considering widening my search to include South America. As it was, I discovered there that the *Atlantic Queen* sailed yesterday, and the *Ocean Monarch* departs tomorrow morning."

"Then it is likely that Baggott will seek to be aboard."

"He must. The next ship sails in five days time, and I doubt if he will choose to risk remaining here for so long. I have advised Lestrade of my discoveries."

"Then I assume we will meet him and his men there tomorrow?"

Holmes nodded. "At 8 o'clock at Royal Victoria Dock."

"Then we remain here until morning?"

"That would be as well, I think." A knowing smile crossed his face. "But I see from your expression and the way you looked at your pocket-watch just now, that you are already hungry. It so happens that I know of a pleasant little place, only a few streets away, that serves excellent food. I keep a bottle of good porter in the kitchen, and after a glass we can be on our way."

"But Holmes," I protested, "are we not here for our safety? Do we not run the risk of encountering Baggott if we leave these premises?"

He blew out a last cloud of fragrant smoke and knocked out his pipe. "The risk of that is now much reduced. While in the dockland area I despatched a further telegram, this time to a young man called Rollins. He is the eldest of the growing crowd of former Irregulars who I have assisted to find employment. When he worked for me his speciality was shadowing people, for I taught him well. I have requested that he watch our lodgings until midnight, and should anyone answering Baggott's description be seen to leave the area he should follow him. If such a person were to arrive in Limehouse, he would be prevented from approaching this house and we would be warned."

"Prevented?" I hoped I had misunderstood my friend's meaning. "Do you mean violently?"

"Not at all." Holmes smiled again. "Rollins would find some way to detain him temporarily. In such matters he is very resourceful. Typical of him would be to represent himself as one of Lestrade's men. He has done this before."

"So you have allowed for Baggott to leave Baker Street in search of us, and also for the eventuality of an assault on our lodgings, since Barker is there also. You appear to have foreseen every development."

"Not quite. We must continue to be on our guard. And now, I will retrieve my bottle of porter, and we will drink before we go out to dine."

We did indeed enjoy a splendid meal, at a small dark restaurant that was well-endowed with customers. The short walk from our hiding-place had been passed with Holmes' eyes in every shadow and in every doorway which could be used for concealment, as was the return later. As he had protected us against every danger, I wondered if he exercised too much caution, then it came to me that Baggott need not, if he had somehow discovered our temporary sanctuary, pursue us in person.

It was late when we returned to our new quarters, but thankfully it was without incident. Holmes insisted that I take the comfortable bed in the upstairs room, while he spent the night on the sitting-room couch. Surprisingly I slept soundly and he seemed none the worse for his experience, as he produced bread and cheese to serve as our breakfast. It was just after seven o'clock when he handed me my hat and coat.

"Are you armed, Watson?"

"As always, my service revolver is to hand."

"Capital! I am also, but it is probably unnecessary with Lestrade in attendance."

My pocket-watch showed that we arrived early at the Royal Victoria Dock. Inspector Lestrade awaited us on the quay, near the steps where a growing queue stood in expectation of the removal of the entrance gate to the loading area. Many sailors attended to their duties in and around the ship, last minute preparations were much in evidence. Their shouts to each other, and the faint hum of conversation from the waiting passengers, were the only sounds except the lapping of water.

"I see that you have your men adequately stationed, Lestrade," Holmes observed.

The official detective scowled. "To anyone but you, Mr Holmes, they would have passed unnoticed."

"I saw them only because I expected to see them. You have placed them as I would have done. The only indication of their concealment is the top of a helmet, showing very slightly above one of those crates near the edge of the quay."

The inspector was about to reply when a uniformed port official climbed the slope and opened the entrance. The waiting crowd surged forward.

Holmes and Lestrade peered keenly at every single person, every couple. I noted the curious variety of souls seeking to leave our shores, each with his or her own reasons, for a new life in a young country. One by one, they filed past us:

Two elderly men, with Southern accents, doubtlessly returning to their own land.

A party of children, in the charge of two women and four men of stern countenance.

A lone man, limping badly.

A bearded middle-aged gentleman, in the company of two younger women. Holmes stared intently at these, but diverted his attention after a few minutes.

A very elderly lady, moving with surprising sprightliness.

A pale young man in a wheelchair, with his nurse. Both Holmes and Lestrade scrutinized these, but only momentarily.

There followed a flood, a tangled mass, of hurrying individuals, couples and occasional groups that were more numerous. Lestrade's eyes were back and forth and he began to appear rather confused, but Holmes allowed his gaze to settle more slowly and with increasing intensity.

"Could you have been mistaken, Mr Holmes?" Lestrade asked after twenty minutes. "Perhaps Baggott realised that you had anticipated him."

"The parade of passengers is not over yet," my friend replied, indicating the trickle that had replaced the initial rush.

The inspector nodded, but said nothing.

A moment later he placed a heavy hand on the shoulder of a rough-looking man who hurried down the slope with his wife, only to remove it and gesture that they should continue.

A fresh crowd of boarders arrived, some of them holding the hand-rail to preserve their balance. Most of them had passed, when Holmes' posture suddenly stiffened like that of a hunting-hound.

"There!" he cried. "Come on, Lestrade!"

The official detective looked in the direction that Holmes had indicated, then ran, blowing his police whistle, to keep pace with Holmes and myself. Many of the queue of passengers stopped and stared in our direction, their attention attracted by the noise and commotion. Two of their number, a man and a woman who had not appeared to be travelling together, immediately attempted to retrace their steps.

They quickly saw that their retreat was blocked by the flood of yet more passengers. They could not pass through the crowd with sufficient speed to allow their escape. Their only option was to forge ahead and they had already begun a frantic run, pushing to one side all that obstructed them.

The man appeared slower than the woman. Lestrade and two of his constables surrounded him and I saw the flash of steel as police handcuffs were produced. As I ran after the woman, trying hard to keep up with Holmes, I heard a strange cry, as of great surprise, from the arresting trio.

The woman sprinted along the dock, knocking over two men who were engaged in loading a large crate. They regained their feet and swore bitterly, but retreating to allow us to pass.

Our quarry looked back at us, over her shoulder. Her travelling-bag, later found to be stuffed with banknotes, fell to the floor. Without stopping, she produced a pistol and fired two rounds. One bullet missed entirely, though I thought Holmes had been hit when he paused for an instant, while the other tore at my coat. From behind us, the heavy footfalls of more of Lestrade's constables grew steadily louder.

Then, in a moment, we all knew that the chase was over.

Before us lay the end of the quay, with only deep water beyond. Another tall ship, the *Atlantic Voyager,* rode the swell and bumped violently against the quayside. As we watched, it buffeted the dock and strained its anchor chains between harsh gusts of the wind that had sprung up.

The woman was obliged to come to a halt, for there was no refuge now.

Both Holmes and I had drawn our firearms.

"Put down your weapon!" my friend shouted. "It is all up with you."

The woman fired twice more, and one of the constables who had now approached cried out.

I fired once, but my shot went astray. The woman ran to the edge of the quay and plunged herself over. Her skirts billowed as the water swallowed her, and we stood watching as she made for the ship. I raised my revolver, although uncertain as to whether I should fire, but Holmes put a hand on my arm.

"It is unnecessary, Watson. Look!"

A strong wind had blown along the quay, forcing the vessels against the dock. I heard an agonised cry, hoarse with terror, and saw blood spread through the saturated skirts as the body was crushed. It vanished instantly.

We replaced our weapons in our pockets as we retraced our steps. I soon determined that the wounded constable was not badly hurt, and the others assisted him as he limped back to where Lestrade and his prisoner waited.

"You appear rather crestfallen, Watson," Holmes remarked as we approached.

"I find it disturbing, to watch a woman die like that."

"That was not a woman."

"What can you mean, Holmes?"

"It was Lester Baggott who, you may remember, we know as a murderer."

"Dressed in women's attire?"

"A means of disguise. He was a hunted man, and he knew it. He and his wife changed identities to confuse pursuit, and to make recognition more difficult."

Certainly my friend was correct. The prisoner, though without rouge or any other feminine feature, was indeed a woman clothed in the attire of a man. She regarded us with a hostile glare, and spat out oaths that raised the constables eyebrows.

"Be quiet!" Lestrade said harshly. "You have a number of charges to answer, and will have the opportunity to speak later."

"As you suspected, Holmes." I remarked as I regarded the ill-dressed woman.

"How did you know, Mr Holmes?" The inspector asked.

"I was quite without hope, after so many had passed us by," Holmes paused as Mrs Baggott was led away. "But when I saw the hands of a woman holding the safety rail while descending the slope, wearing *a man's wedding ring,* I knew at once that here was someone hiding their true identity. Then it was a matter of calling out, and observing the response."

"My compliments to you," Lestrade said then, "for your assistance to Scotland Yard on this matter."

Holmes looked at the official detective in a way that I had seen many times before. "My trifling contribution may have enhanced the outcome of this affair to some small extent, Inspector, but I am glad to think that it will add to your record of commendable successes."

"Then it is likely that Baggott will seek to be aboard."

"He must. The next ship sails in five days time, and I doubt if he will choose to risk remaining here for so long. I have advised Lestrade of my discoveries."

"Then I assume we will meet him and his men there tomorrow?"

Holmes nodded. "At 8 o'clock at Royal Victoria Dock."

"Then we remain here until morning?"

"That would be as well, I think." A knowing smile crossed his face. "But I see from your expression and the way you looked at your pocket-watch just now, that you are already hungry. It so happens that I know of a pleasant little place, only a few streets away, that serves excellent food. I keep a bottle of good porter in the kitchen, and after a glass we can be on our way."

"But Holmes," I protested, "are we not here for our safety? Do we not run the risk of encountering Baggott if we leave these premises?"

He blew out a last cloud of fragrant smoke and knocked out his pipe. "The risk of that is now much reduced. While in the dockland area I despatched a further telegram, this time to a young man called Rollins. He is the eldest of the growing crowd of former Irregulars who I have assisted to find employment. When he worked for me his speciality was shadowing people, for I taught him well. I have requested that he watch our lodgings until midnight, and should anyone answering Baggott's description be seen to leave the area he should follow him. If such a person were to arrive in Limehouse, he would be prevented from approaching this house and we would be warned."

"Prevented?" I hoped I had misunderstood my friend's meaning. "Do you mean violently?"

"Not at all." Holmes smiled again. "Rollins would find some way to detain him temporarily. In such matters he is very resourceful. Typical of him would be to represent himself as one of Lestrade's men. He has done this before."

"So you have allowed for Baggott to leave Baker Street in search of us, and also for the eventuality of an assault on our lodgings, since Barker is there also. You appear to have foreseen every development."

"Not quite. We must continue to be on our guard. And now, I will retrieve my bottle of porter, and we will drink before we go out to dine."

We did indeed enjoy a splendid meal, at a small dark restaurant that was well-endowed with customers. The short walk from our hiding-place had been passed with Holmes' eyes in every shadow and in every doorway which could be used for concealment, as was the return later. As he had protected us against every danger, I wondered if he exercised too much caution, then it came to me that Baggott need not, if he had somehow discovered our temporary sanctuary, pursue us in person.

It was late when we returned to our new quarters, but thankfully it was without incident. Holmes insisted that I take the comfortable bed in the upstairs room, while he spent the night on the sitting-room couch. Surprisingly I slept soundly and he seemed none the worse for his experience, as he produced bread and cheese to serve as our breakfast. It was just after seven o'clock when he handed me my hat and coat.

"Are you armed, Watson?"

"As always, my service revolver is to hand."

"Capital! I am also, but it is probably unnecessary with Lestrade in attendance."

My pocket-watch showed that we arrived early at the Royal Victoria Dock. Inspector Lestrade awaited us on the quay, near the steps where a growing queue stood in expectation of the removal of the entrance gate to the loading area. Many sailors attended to their duties in and around the ship, last minute preparations were much in evidence. Their shouts to each other, and the faint hum of conversation from the waiting passengers, were the only sounds except the lapping of water.

"I see that you have your men adequately stationed, Lestrade," Holmes observed.

The official detective scowled. "To anyone but you, Mr Holmes, they would have passed unnoticed."

"I saw them only because I expected to see them. You have placed them as I would have done. The only indication of their concealment is the top of a helmet, showing very slightly above one of those crates near the edge of the quay."

The inspector was about to reply when a uniformed port official climbed the slope and opened the entrance. The waiting crowd surged forward.

Holmes and Lestrade peered keenly at every single person, every couple. I noted the curious variety of souls seeking to leave our shores, each with his or her own reasons, for a new life in a young country. One by one, they filed past us:

Two elderly men, with Southern accents, doubtlessly returning to their own land.

A party of children, in the charge of two women and four men of stern countenance.

A lone man, limping badly.

A bearded middle-aged gentleman, in the company of two younger women. Holmes stared intently at these, but diverted his attention after a few minutes.

A very elderly lady, moving with surprising sprightliness.

A pale young man in a wheelchair, with his nurse. Both Holmes and Lestrade scrutinized these, but only momentarily.

There followed a flood, a tangled mass, of hurrying individuals, couples and occasional groups that were more numerous. Lestrade's eyes were back and forth and he began to appear rather confused, but Holmes allowed his gaze to settle more slowly and with increasing intensity.

"Could you have been mistaken, Mr Holmes?" Lestrade asked after twenty minutes. "Perhaps Baggott realised that you had anticipated him."

"The parade of passengers is not over yet," my friend replied, indicating the trickle that had replaced the initial rush.

The inspector nodded, but said nothing.

A moment later he placed a heavy hand on the shoulder of a rough-looking man who hurried down the slope with his wife, only to remove it and gesture that they should continue.

A fresh crowd of boarders arrived, some of them holding the hand-rail to preserve their balance. Most of them had passed, when Holmes' posture suddenly stiffened like that of a hunting-hound.

"There!" he cried. "Come on, Lestrade!"

The official detective looked in the direction that Holmes had indicated, then ran, blowing his police whistle, to keep pace with Holmes and myself. Many of the queue of passengers stopped and stared in our direction, their attention attracted by the noise and commotion. Two of their number, a man and a woman who had not appeared to be travelling together, immediately attempted to retrace their steps.

They quickly saw that their retreat was blocked by the flood of yet more passengers. They could not pass through the crowd with sufficient speed to allow their escape. Their only option was to forge ahead and they had already begun a frantic run, pushing to one side all that obstructed them.

The man appeared slower than the woman. Lestrade and two of his constables surrounded him and I saw the flash of steel as police handcuffs were produced. As I ran after the woman, trying hard to keep up with Holmes, I heard a strange cry, as of great surprise, from the arresting trio.

The woman sprinted along the dock, knocking over two men who were engaged in loading a large crate. They regained their feet and swore bitterly, but retreating to allow us to pass.

Our quarry looked back at us, over her shoulder. Her travelling-bag, later found to be stuffed with banknotes, fell to the floor. Without stopping, she produced a pistol and fired two rounds. One bullet missed entirely, though I thought Holmes had been hit when he paused for an instant, while the other tore at my coat. From behind us, the heavy footfalls of more of Lestrade's constables grew steadily louder.

Then, in a moment, we all knew that the chase was over.

Before us lay the end of the quay, with only deep water beyond. Another tall ship, the *Atlantic Voyager,* rode the swell and bumped violently against the quayside. As we watched, it buffeted the dock and strained its anchor chains between harsh gusts of the wind that had sprung up.

The woman was obliged to come to a halt, for there was no refuge now.

Both Holmes and I had drawn our firearms.

"Put down your weapon!" my friend shouted. "It is all up with you."

The woman fired twice more, and one of the constables who had now approached cried out.

I fired once, but my shot went astray. The woman ran to the edge of the quay and plunged herself over. Her skirts billowed as the water swallowed her, and we stood watching as she made for the ship. I raised my revolver, although uncertain as to whether I should fire, but Holmes put a hand on my arm.

"It is unnecessary, Watson. Look!"

A strong wind had blown along the quay, forcing the vessels against the dock. I heard an agonised cry, hoarse with terror, and saw blood spread through the saturated skirts as the body was crushed. It vanished instantly.

We replaced our weapons in our pockets as we retraced our steps. I soon determined that the wounded constable was not badly hurt, and the others assisted him as he limped back to where Lestrade and his prisoner waited.

"You appear rather crestfallen, Watson," Holmes remarked as we approached.

"I find it disturbing, to watch a woman die like that."

"That was not a woman."

"What can you mean, Holmes?"

"It was Lester Baggott who, you may remember, we know as a murderer."

"Dressed in women's attire?"

"A means of disguise. He was a hunted man, and he knew it. He and his wife changed identities to confuse pursuit, and to make recognition more difficult."

Certainly my friend was correct. The prisoner, though without rouge or any other feminine feature, was indeed a woman clothed in the attire of a man. She regarded us with a hostile glare, and spat out oaths that raised the constables eyebrows.

"Be quiet!" Lestrade said harshly. "You have a number of charges to answer, and will have the opportunity to speak later."

"As you suspected, Holmes." I remarked as I regarded the ill-dressed woman.

"How did you know, Mr Holmes?" The inspector asked.

"I was quite without hope, after so many had passed us by," Holmes paused as Mrs Baggott was led away. "But when I saw the hands of a woman holding the safety rail while descending the slope, wearing *a man's wedding ring,* I knew at once that here was someone hiding their true identity. Then it was a matter of calling out, and observing the response."

"My compliments to you," Lestrade said then, "for your assistance to Scotland Yard on this matter."

Holmes looked at the official detective in a way that I had seen many times before. "My trifling contribution may have enhanced the outcome of this affair to some small extent, Inspector, but I am glad to think that it will add to your record of commendable successes."

The Adventure of the Unknown Traitor

Of all the eccentricities of my friend Mr Sherlock Holmes that I became accustomed to during our long association, I always considered his aversion to exercise for its own sake the least understandable. It was with some surprise therefore, that I accepted his invitation to accompany him on a stroll in The Regents Park immediately after breakfast one frosty March morning.

Clad in our heavy coats and wearing scarves and gloves, we walked along glistening paths still strewn with the leaves of last autumn, beneath skeletal trees that waited to again burst into life. The freezing air stung our faces. We spoke little, not unusually for him, but something of a rarity for myself. I knew of course that Holmes would quickly notice my reticence, for his powers had not noticeably declined over the years, and so his enquiry as we regained the streets of the capital was not unexpected.

"What is troubling you, Watson?" he asked as we waited for a landau to pass before crossing the road. 'You have spoken hardly a word since we left Baker Street.'

"I am caught on the horns of a dilemma."

He laughed shortly. "I deduced as much. After reading the fourth letter in your post after breakfast, your mood changed instantly. It goes without saying, old fellow, that I am at your disposal to assist if you find yourself in difficulty."

"I am exceedingly glad to hear that, Holmes, for no one else could aid my decision."

"Then pray enlighten me. Beginning with the letter, tell me all."

The morning crowds grew thicker as we approached the West End. Young men in particular strode purposefully past us after dismissing their transportation, presumably late in attending their employment. Holmes nimbly avoided a young and, I thought, probably inexperienced nanny pushing a perambulator at a fast rate. He apologised with his usual good manners before I answered.

"It was a communication that I did not expect. The sender was an old army comrade, Carlton Ferrers."

He nodded. "But why has it caused you such apparent anxiety?"

"For the first time since my army days, I am invited to a meeting with him and three other survivors."

"I would have thought the renewal of old friendships a pleasant experience. Where is the dilemma?"

I half-turned to see his expression and gauge his response. "My dilemma was whether or not to put this to you. Ferrers specifies that you should accompany me, if that is possible."

"Could that be because he anticipates a need for my services?"

"That is what I surmised," I shrugged. "But I have not seen these men for some years, and know nothing of their lives since Maiwand."

A beggar, wrapped in an old blanket and visibly shivering, staggered across our path and hesitated as he decided whether to accost us. Before he could speak, Holmes dropped some coins into his tin cup and he mumbled his thanks.

"Poor fellow," I said.

"Indeed. Tell me, were these men particular friends of yours?"

"Not at all. They were unknown to me, apart from our service. You could say that the war threw us together."

"When is this gathering to be?"

"Tomorrow evening at eight o'clock. A room has been reserved at the Langham Hotel."

I saw his expression lighten. "Very well, Watson. I confess to having become curious about this. I will accompany you, as you have me on so many occasions. How are you to notify Mr Ferrers, as he now is, of your acceptance?"

"He requested that I do so by telegraph, at his address in Kent."

"I see that we are almost in Baker Street, and just ahead is a hansom that has just delivered its fare. I suggest that you procure it to get to the nearest Post Office from where you can send your message. On your return to our rooms I think a brandy is in order, to dispel this infernal chill that seems to be worsening by the minute."

#

Less than half an hour later, we sat in our usual armchairs on either side of our sitting-room fireplace. As he had promised, Holmes had already poured the brandy, and it was only after the restorative effect of the fiery spirit that he referred to the matter again.

"Tell me," he said as we replaced our empty glasses, "all that you know of these men. It may provide some notion of what to expect, tomorrow night."

I leaned back in my chair and searched my memory. "To the best of my recollection they were part of a larger group. Our detachment sent out an expeditionary force when we were camped three days out of Kandahar. We were to meet some of our spies from

Ayub Khan's forces, who were to tell us of his intended movements, but something went horribly wrong. In the darkness there was chaos, with gunfire all around and men dropping like flies. The remnants of our party arrived back at camp eventually and we made our reports, after I had done what I could for the wounded survivors. The following day we arrived at the Maiwand Pass where, as you know, we were defeated and I received my wounds."

"Quite so." Holmes spent a few minutes in quiet thought, before adding: "Well, I expect we will discover your former comrades' intentions tomorrow night. For now, I see that you have yet to complete your notes on the cases you mentioned yesterday, while I have a chemical experiment in progress that could save Jason Morrell from the gallows. We have two hours before luncheon, and after that I have a promise to keep. One of my informants is appearing in an appalling drama at the Lyceum, and I am quite certain that she would be doubly gratified if you were to attend also."

#

I spent most of the following day with a dying patient who, in late afternoon, took an unexpected turn for the better. On returning to our lodgings I found Holmes seated on our sitting-room floor, surrounded by several open volumes of his index.

"Ah, Watson," he said, looking up. "Allow me a moment or two to replace all this and we can indulge ourselves in an early dinner. I have informed Mrs Hudson of our plans for tonight."

For once, Holmes did justice to Mrs Hudson's steak and kidney pie. For my part I enjoyed it as ever. No sooner was our meal concluded than he selected a book from the shelf. I saw that he was consulting *Who's Who*, and surmised that he searched for information about my former comrades. At length he replaced the volume and handed me my hat and coat. Minutes later, both wrapped up against the cold, we left our lodgings.

The pavement twinkled as the evening grew colder and the frost returned. Thankfully a hansom appeared quickly, and the short distance to the Langham Hotel was traversed without incident. We passed from Regent Street into Portland Place and left our conveyance near the entrance of our destination. The fellow at the reception desk, on learning of our purpose there, called a uniformed boy to show us to a small conference room. He accepted Holmes' tip and opened the heavy door for us to enter.

The room, panelled in dark wood, was lit by a candelabra at each end of a long table. Four men sat around it, each looking in our direction. I noticed that there were two empty chairs, and that a carafe of water and a glass stood untouched by each place. Like ourselves, each man wore evening attire, and in a moment I recognised my old comrades, despite the changes that the years had wreaked upon them.

No one spoke until the door closed. Then a man carrying rather more weight than I remembered got to his feet.

"Mr Holmes, Doctor Watson. Welcome, and thank you for attending. It was I whose letter you received at Baker Street. I am Carlton Ferrers."

We both gave a small bow in acknowledgement.

"Thank you for the invitation, Mr Ferrers," Holmes answered, "Whatever your difficulty, I am at your disposal."

Ferrers at once became embarrassed. "My thanks, sir. I have asked my former three comrades here under a deception. This is not to be simply a reunion, but hopefully the occasion when a mystery that has lain heavily on my mind since our days in Afghanistan is finally made clear."

I saw that the other three at the table had begun looking at each other in surprise.

"Be seated and hear me out," Ferrers invited us, "I beg of you."

There was a moment of complete silence, and Holmes' expression gave no indication of his thoughts. I confess to my curiosity as to Ferrer's purpose.

"Very well, although I fail to understand how anything arising from that war can be my concern," my friend remarked.

"After my explanation, you will realise that the presence of a man of undisputed integrity is necessary to conclude the matter. Watson was an obvious choice, the more so because of his association with yourself."

Ferrers looked relieved as we took our seats. I introduced my friend to the remaining three men.

"Mr Godfrey Stone, Mr Henry Gillespie, Mr Harcourt Vernon, my former comrades in the Second Anglo-Afghan War - Mr Sherlock Holmes."

Holmes acknowledged them, and they responded with nods and mumbled greetings. I studied each man briefly. Ferrers appeared heavier, as did they all, and age had turned his hair and beard white. Stone had lost much of the shock of red hair of his youth, while Gillespie had added a magnificent handlebar moustache to his gaunt features. Vernon alone seemed closest to my recollection of him, except that his face was now excessively flushed. I wondered if his heart was ailing then decided that this was probably true, since his eyes repeatedly wandered to the water carafe. He wished it, willed it, to be magically transformed to a flask of whisky or brandy. I had seen that look many times before, in patients long addicted to strong drink.

"I believe our group was more numerous," I remarked.

"Indeed it was," Gillespie remembered. "I have kept track of some of the others since the battle. Mullins, Inman and Updike fell in engagements subsequent to Maiwand, and McBride, Quirner and O'Fallon died since from various natural causes."

A momentary wave of regret swept over me, as I recalled these men as they had once been.

"I assume then that this mystery, as you have called it, originates either before, during or immediately after you gentlemen served in Afghanistan," Holmes ventured. "If I am to assist in any way, I must have the facts. Reasoning is impossible without them."

"I cannot imagine how there can be any question attached to the affair," Vernon retorted. "I have no recollection of anything except gunfire and death."

"Nor I," Stone agreed.

"To refresh your memories if need be, and for Mr Holmes' information, I will relate what occurred on the day before the Battle of Maiwand," Ferrers began. "Should my own recollection be less than accurate, I am sure that Doctor Watson will correct me. Assuming, that is, that his memory retains the accuracy of his youth." He smiled faintly and paused to glance at the others, who remained silent.

"Pray continue," Holmes urged with a trace of impatience.

Ferrers shifted in his chair. "You will recall, at the very least, that three days after leaving Kandahar we were to join the main forces of Brigadier-General George Burrows to engage those of Ayub Khan. Our group, comprising twenty-five men, were sent out from the camp at night, to meet and obtain information from paid spies from within his ranks."

"An appalling mess," Stone said quietly.

"Quite," Ferrers allowed, "for we met a detachment of Khan's forces and were taken by surprise. In the slaughter that followed, fifteen of our men lost their lives. We always believed the incident to have been a chance encounter, but I now have reason to suspect otherwise."

He broke off to pour himself water, and then drained his glass. I saw that a curious expression had crept onto the faces of the others.

"I should explain," Ferrers resumed, "that I decided some time ago to write a memoir of my military experiences. I journeyed back to Kandahar, and to the nearby villages from where our guides and assistants were drawn. After considerable effort I found some of them, now much older of course, who were willing to talk at length to me of the events that transpired on the eve of the battle and the days after. It was during this research that I realised the truth of that fateful night."

"What can you mean, Ferrers?" Gillespie asked.

"My meaning, and the true purpose of this gathering, will become abundantly clear, when I tell you that I discovered and proved beyond doubt that we were betrayed. Khan's soldiers were waiting, ready to destroy us, not by chance or circumstance but because one of our own had informed them of our intended liaison with the spies who, incidentally, were executed after torture."

Now, the other three became visibly uncomfortable. Each looked at the others suspiciously and shock was written on all their faces. The atmosphere in the room seemed to cool.

"Your purpose tonight then," Holmes said, breaking the silence that had fallen on the room by addressing Ferrers, "is to unmask the traitor, presumably?"

"Indeed. This has occupied my every waking moment since I saw the truth of the situation."

"It will have occurred to you that the traitor could have been one of those comrades who later died in other battles, or even those who survived to meet a natural end?"

Ferrers nodded. "My first task was to ascertain the innocence of the dead by further research. I succeeded eventually. I confess to being appalled and saddened to conclude that the man who betrayed the company can only be one of the remaining comrades. One of the three with me at this table, now."

The effect on the others ranged from dismay to anger. Stone, white-faced, said nothing.

"This is preposterous!" Vernon exclaimed. "How can you tell? It was all so long ago."

Gillespie shook his head slowly. "I wouldn't trust those natives for your information. They'd sell their souls for a few coins."

"They were not my only source," Ferrers replied.

Vernon and Gillespie got to their feet.

"I will not sit here and listen to this piffle!" Vernon said loudly.

"Nor I," added Gillespie. "The past is dead, that war is part of the history of each of us and cannot be changed. I say leave it, and let us all leave this place."

Both men made to move from their positions at the table, but Ferrers would have none of it.

"Resume your seats at once!" he ordered in the sharp voice that I remembered from his service as a colonel at Maiwand. Then, more calmly, "In any case, Gentlemen, I have requested that the door be kept locked for the duration of our occupancy. Kindly be seated again."

173

They obeyed reluctantly. Holmes, I saw, had remained impassive.

"I see now why they need someone neutral but known to them," I said to him in a low voice. "In this situation, not one can trust the others. How do you think we should proceed, or should we leave?"

My friend adopted a thoughtful expression, but decided in a moment.

"Gentlemen," he began, glancing at each in turn, "I cannot doubt that you are men of honour."

There was a unanimous murmur of assent.

"Excellent. I have a suggestion which is extreme, but will permanently remedy the mistrust and shame that one of you has brought upon your group and your regiment." He took a revolver from his pocket, emptied the chambers and put away the bullets. From a waistcoat pocket he produced a single bullet which he loaded into the weapon. "If guilty, an honourable man will recognise that there is but one way out, that of atonement. Then all will be clear and the doubt in the minds of his comrades will be erased. I propose that I leave my revolver here," he slid it to the centre of the table, "so that the guilty man can make use of it. Watson will extinguish the candles at the far end of the table and I the other, at precisely the same instant. When the report is heard the light will be immediately restored, otherwise the candles will be re-lit when, by my calculation, three minutes have passed." He again glanced at each face. "Are we all agreed?"

A babble of outrage commenced immediately, but was short-lived. The others, appearing confused and, I thought, a little afraid, stared at Ferrers as if for guidance. The silence that fell upon the room then did not last.

"I think Mister Holmes' suggestion most appropriate," the former colonel judged, "and compassionate inasmuch as it allows for the traitor to retain a semblance of honour by adopting a manly course. That should spare the shame of his relatives and dependents somewhat."

They responded with reluctant sounds, like tortured breaths, which were taken as the agreement of each man. This plan seemed far from secure, and I glanced at my friend doubtfully, but his answering look told me that, as always, he had considered every likely outcome already.

All eyes were fixed on Holmes' weapon, as if it were a venomous serpent, as he rose and moved to the end of the table. I left my seat, and from the opposite end looked past them all while awaiting Holmes' signal.

Silence descended again, and it came to me that the guilty man must be suffering agonies of fear and indecision at this moment. Then my friend extinguished every candle near to him, some with a large snuffer and the remainder with a mighty exhalation. I tried twice, before achieving the same effect.

Because the windows were heavily-curtained, the darkness was complete. Faint movements, I could not tell from exactly where, disturbed the silence. A coldness, like that within a tomb, seemed to envelop me, and I told myself that the time limit must surely expire in an instant. Then a cry of fearful surprise was immediately followed by the flare of a vesta as Holmes re-lit the candles, after which I did likewise to those in the candelabra before me.

Everyone blinked and looked around cautiously as the scene was again illuminated. From Holmes' expression, I knew that he had learned from the situation.

The revolver was now in the hand of Ferrers, but he appeared confused, rather than guilty.

"I did not pick it up," he stammered. "My word on it. Someone forced the weapon into my hand and tried to press it to my head."

"And in another moment you would have appeared to have taken your own life," Holmes concluded. "it would be forever thought that you yourself were the traitor." His glance took in the table. "His task would have been easier had the traitor shot you before throwing the weapon down, but would have been easier also for me to deduce his identity. Evidently, he realised this."

"Yes," said Ferrers, still somewhat dazed by this unexpected event. "I suppose that must have been the intention." He gave the others a curious look. "Thank you, Mr Holmes."

"Well, whatever that little demonstration was intended to prove, it failed miserably," Stone commented.

Holmes shook his head. "Much to the contrary, it proved exactly the one point about which I was uncertain."

"And what might that have been?" asked Vernon.

"That Mr Ferrers was correct when he stated that the traitor was not among the dead of your group. Had that been so, none of you here would have found it necessary to make it appear that he himself is the guilty man."

"Whose true identity we have failed to establish," observed Gillespie.

"Only as yet," I corrected. "Mr Holmes rarely fails to expose the truth, in the end."

"Do you realise the needless danger you placed us in with this?" Vernon asked Holmes. "Any one of us could have accidentally handled that revolver, and it could have fired unintentionally in the darkness causing injury or death."

"Not so, I assure you. It may have occurred to you to wonder why I emptied the weapon and then produced another bullet for the experiment, if we may call it that, when I could simply have left one of the original bullets in the chamber and proceeded from there. The bullet I used had remained in my waistcoat pocket, forgotten from a previous affair, and it was on discovering it that the idea came to me. There was no possibility of injury because, for another purpose entirely, I had previously removed the gunpowder."

"You are telling us that, if the guilty man had attempted to kill himself, he could not have done so?" Stone enquired with some surprise.

"It would have been impossible, but he would have identified himself, and all that remained would have been to notify Scotland Yard."

"Would his actions in Afghanistan still be considered a crime?" Gillespie asked.

"That would be for the courts to decide, of course. At the very least, he would be considered a pariah by all who know him."

Ferrers seemed to have recovered himself by now.

"But unfortunately, we have failed to establish his identity after all," he said. "Mr Holmes, I must apologise for arranging for you to attend an occasion that has been fraught with failure. Please feel free to send me your account, for your attempt was indeed ingenious."

Holmes rose, and I followed.

"That will not be necessary, Mr Ferrers," my friend responded. "Nor is this incident concluded. If you will make the arrangements with the hotel, and you gentlemen are free, I propose that we meet here again at the same time on the evening after tomorrow. I have every reason to expect that I will be able to throw light upon the situation by then."

Ferrers, appearing eager to comply with Holmes' suggestion, turned to the others. Stone nodded his agreement at once, but Gillespie merely shrugged. Vernon smiled faintly for the first time and raised a hand to concur.

"Very well," Ferrers said a little wearily.

"Then if you will summon someone to open the door, Doctor Watson and I will be on our way."

#

I breakfasted alone the next morning. Holmes, I knew because the teapot was cold, had eaten some time previously. Mrs Hudson informed me that he had said it was unlikely that he would return until dinner-time.

My practice was unusually busy that day, but most of my patients suffered from minor ailments only. I arrived back at Baker Street in the late afternoon, and drank a welcome glass of port while attending to my neglected notes.

Dinner-time came and went. I enjoyed our landlady's excellent game pie, while expecting the arrival of my friend at any moment. To my disappointment he failed to appear, and I had been settled in my armchair reading for several hours before I heard his tread upon the stair. He burst into the room with blood on his face, and suffering obvious pain.

"Holmes!" I cried. "Good heavens, what has happened to you?"

He sat down awkwardly. "I was attacked. I believe that one of your former comrades intended that I should not complete my investigation."

"Are you certain that they were connected with this incident," I enquired as I helped him remove his coat. "I will call Mrs Hudson to bring hot water."

"So much ado is not necessary, Watson. My body is bruised from receiving several blows from a stout stick, but the cut on my face is slight. There were two of them, but I'll wager they came off worst."

Our landlady responded to my request nevertheless, and I tended to Holmes' wounds with him complaining throughout.

"Why are you so certain that your attackers were sent by one of my old comrades?" I asked again when my examination was over and we each held a glass of brandy.

"I can think of no one else likely to be responsible. The Marrason brothers are behind bars awaiting trial, Miss Shirley Christopher has begun a long sentence in Holloway and, according to today's *Standard,* Morton Chiles has committed suicide. As you will recall, I have had no more recent cases."

"You were not able to learn anything from either of your assailants?"

"I was not, regrettably. They came at me out of the shadows near Tottenham Court Road, where I had led them after discovering that I was being followed. They were men of considerable size, but not too skilful or intelligent. I left one of them bleeding from a stomach punctured by my sword-stick and the other, I suspect, with a broken arm."

"Will you tell Lestrade?"

"Possibly, but I think that will have little effect. I am aware of their usual haunts, should their arrest prove necessary."

"Have you made any progress towards learning the identity of the traitor in Afghanistan?"

"I have identified him as the only one of your former comrades that could have betrayed your regiment."

"So quickly?" I retorted in surprise. "How did you accomplish that, Holmes?"

He took a final sip of his brandy and replaced his glass on a side-table. "Let me tell you how my day was spent." He smiled faintly. "You may be able to include the incidents in one of your over-dramatised accounts of my little enquiries, someday."

I had long since become accustomed to his remarks concerning my work, so I made no reply.

"Kindly proceed," I said encouragingly. Fortunately my note-book was close at hand, and I retrieved it as he leaned back in his chair and began his reminiscences with closed eyes.

"As you will be aware, I left Baker Street after an early breakfast. My intention was to arrive at Whitehall before Mycroft began his daily routine, in the hope that he would spare me sufficient time to arrange access to the National Archives. He was not pleased to see me, but I was able to persuade him of the importance of the matter and he eventually complied. Once installed in that labyrinth I was able to search at my leisure, sometimes with the assistance of the resident curator, and the records of your comrades' actions, as far as they are known, were discovered. When all was known I left the establishment, suddenly aware that it was now late in the day. As I neared our lodgings I came to realise that another hansom had followed my conveyance for about the last half mile, so I directed my driver to Tottenham Court Road, where I took to walking and led my persuers a merry dance until they attacked me. When that unpleasant incident had passed, I engaged another hansom to bring me back here."

"I wish I had been with you," I said sincerely. "Those roughs might have inflicted less damage, against two of us."

"Good old Watson. I confess to believing that I had eluded them, but at least one must know the streets there as well as I. It was a surprise attack but, as I have explained, I was able to prevail."

The question on my lips was of course the identity of my traitorous former comrade, but I knew that Holmes would reveal nothing until the second meeting of tomorrow night. I was about to suggest that he retire early because of his exertions, when he stood up to stretch his thin body and announce that this was his intention. Left alone, I read one of my accumulated medical journals, before taking to my bed.

#

Holmes had not risen by breakfast-time, so once more I ate alone. My day was spent treating several seriously ill patients and on some little time at Barts, before I was able to return to Baker Street. As I approached our lodgings I saw a tall, serious-faced elderly man emerge, and wondered what new problem my friend had been confronted with during my absence.

"Nothing to occupy me for long," he informed me when we were seated and awaiting Mrs Hudson's entrance with our dinner. "I had the unenviable task of revealing to Mr Oliver Fortesque-Jones that the much younger woman he was about to marry is actually his estranged daughter of many years. The poor fellow was so shocked that I found it necessary to refill his brandy glass several times. He had apparently almost forgotten the original marriage of his youth."

"That is an incredible situation!" I exclaimed.

"Indeed, but it is not unique. Remind me to tell you of Miss Isabelle Coultier and the circus clown, a small matter that I was presented with whilst living in Montague Street, when we have a moment to ourselves. It was a farce that might prove amusing to your readers. Today's enquiry however, was conducted entirely within this room." He inclined his head towards the door. "Ah, but I hear our good landlady on the stairs. The accompanying aroma tells me that we are about to partake of some excellent fish, and after that we must discuss briefly what is to take place at the Langham Hotel."

#

To a man, we all arrived early for the second meeting. When we were seated as before I scrutinized the face of each of my former comrades, but learned nothing. Every countenance showed strain and anticipation. I wondered how many memories of that bloody war of yesteryear would be shattered by the exposure of unexpected truths.

"This will not take up much of our time," Holmes began when he was certain that he had their attention, "and then, in the light of the truth, the blameless ones among you will be exonerated."

I saw that Ferrers' gaze remained on him, while the remaining three regarded each other nervously. The candles flickered, projecting a shadow on each man's expression that lent a sinister air. Vernon, I thought, looked paler than before.

"The guilty man stands accused of conveying vital information, in this case of the movements of your expeditionary force, to the enemy," my friend continued. "To do this, he had to have been absent from your camp for some little time immediately before the mission began, and after the orders were issued. My method of procedure therefore, was to consult the official records of the actions of each of you at the time and the journal of your immediate commanding officer."

"You were able to gain access to such information, so quickly?" Ferrers asked incredulously.

"Indeed. The results of my research were surprising."

Concern was etched into the faces of Stone, Gillespie and Vernon. Each radiated guilt, and I wondered if Holmes had uncovered a conspiracy. Ferrers, I saw, was aware of their uneasiness.

"I will begin with Mr Gillespie," Holmes paused as the man fiddled nervously with his moustache, "who is exonerated from this charge since he had been confined to his quarters for several days." Gillespie stared at the table-top, unable to meet our eyes. "The records are rather vague concerning the reason, but it is clear that it involved his actions towards a local girl and the resulting dispute with her family."

All eyes were now on Gillespie, who shook his head slowly but made no comment.

"With Mr Stone it was different," Holmes revealed then. "According to the daily journal he was at that time secretly involved with the exposure of those among the native bearers who sold opium to the servicemen. Unfortunately, he was found to have accepted payment from the offenders rather than to be instrumental in their arrest. Hardly commendable, but once again it does exclude him from the charge of betrayal."

"It was never proven," Stone protested. "Sergeant Brooker wrote down his opinion, that was all. The man disliked me from the beginning."

Ferrers fixed both Gillespie and Stone with a frosty glance, and said simply, "You disappoint me," but the effect on their expressions was as if they had received a whipping.

"And so," Holmes concluded, "we are left with you, Mr Vernon. At first I could see no opportunity when you could have conversed with the enemy, but then I discovered that you volunteered to ride out to search for and bring back to camp a certain Private McLellan. Apparently the poor fellow had previously suffered some sort of mental blackout and wandered off unobserved. The Sergeant's journal mentions surprise that you were away for so long, and regret that McLellan was dead when you caught up with him."

Vernon was now visibly agitated. He turned his head this way and that, but there was no avoiding the contemptuous glares of every man in the room.

"I didn't want to do it," he said in a voice that shook with fear, "but I was desperate. My run of bad luck at the tables before we left England had put me in deep debt. I knew what I would have to face when the war was over and we returned home, and I could see no way out until one of the bearers offered me a solution. He arranged for me to meet Ayub Khan's man with the information." He paused, his tone heavy with shame. "When I had disclosed it, the money was thrown at my feet and the man turned and rode off abruptly."

"No one has respect for a traitor," Ferrers said in a voice that surprised me with its deadly calmness. "You do realise how many of your comrades died, because of you?"

"There is one thing more," Holmes added before Vernon could reply. "The journal recounts that McLellan was dead when you returned to the camp. Since there was no obvious cause," he held Vernon's eyes and spoke in a harsh but level voice, "the eventual verdict was that he died of exposure, but is the truth that you killed him because he witnessed the meeting?"

Vernon appeared shocked, and I wondered if this was because he considered Holmes' supposition to be outrageous, or because the final discovery of his act was unexpected. His pallor was now darker than before, and a violent trembling had come upon him.

"Also," my friend continued, "I should mention that the two blackguards who you sent to silence me last night were totally incompetent. It is to be hoped that they put you to no great expense."

Receiving no answer, Holmes turned to make a remark to Ferrers as Vernon made a frenzied dash for the door at the instant his glance was averted. On reaching it and discovering that it held fast against his attempts to wrench it open, he beat upon it while beginning to stagger and cry out hysterically.

Holmes, Ferrers and myself were across the room quickly, and my friend caught Vernon before his body hit the ground. I saw at once that the immense strain and the years of strong drink that he had used to numb the pain of his guilt had taken the ultimate toll.

"The end of an evening that has been far from the finest in the regiment's history," Ferrers said somewhat sadly. "Was it his heart, Doctor?"

"I am sure that an examination will prove so," I agreed. "He could bear his burden no longer."

"He is beyond the vengeance that I see written on your faces," Holmes told the others. "While this is understandable, I could not allow it. As I had no way of predicting Vernon's death, I took the precaution of arranging for Inspector Lestrade of Scotland Yard to attend for the arrest. Possibly his journey has not been entirely wasted, since he may require a few words with Mr Stone. If you would signal for the door to be opened, Mr Ferrers, I believe you will find that he is waiting."

My recollection is that our conversation with the inspector was over quite quickly, and of Ferrers voicing his appreciation of Holmes' efforts once more before we left.

"I'm sorry, Holmes," I said to break the silence shortly after, as our cab neared Baker Street.

"Whatever for, old fellow?"

"I meant for involving you in that sorry affair."

"Its conclusion brought no satisfaction it is true, but the truth needed to be exposed. You must have wondered how it was that your group's foray was expected, that night all those years ago."

"It is not a recollection that I dwell upon often."

"Nor would I. However, it is getting late and I am expecting a client with a most intriguing tale to tell, to be at our door in the morning. I therefore suggest that, after a restorative beverage in our sitting-room, we retire a little earlier than usual."

The Adventure of the Serpent's Head

It was, as I recall, about a month after Holmes' return from his long absence that we settled into our armchairs after breakfast in order that he could fulfil his promise to me. This was that he would relate some of his experiences in foreign parts, for he knew well that I was eager to hear of his adventures.

We had lit cigars, and he leaned back in his chair and blew smoke rings into the air. I could see from his expression that he was formulating a narrative in his mind, possibly with a view to excluding certain incidents which, for reasons of his own, he did not wish to disclose.

"You did promise, Holmes," I prompted, "even if you mentioned that some of your revelations would not be permitted for publication."

"Quite so. My hesitation is merely to use a few minutes to assemble the facts in the manner which you will find most interesting."

I put aside my cigar and prepared to listen to my friend's exploits. He took a final puff and ground the remnants of his tobacco into an ashtray. Through the cloud of smoke surrounding him I saw that he had settled on the form that his presentation was to take and was about to begin. With my notebook poised, I leaned forward with great anticipation.

At that moment, the door-bell rang.

We immediately allowed silence to fall between us, straining our ears to hear the conversation between Mrs Hudson, our landlady, and our visitor.

"It may be the butcher's boy," I suggested, hoping that the caller was not about to interrupt our conversation.

Holmes shook his head. "No, Watson, it is a young lady, and Mrs Hudson is already leading her up the stairs to us. I am afraid that my experiences that you are so keen to hear about will have to wait, for now."

Inwardly, I scowled, but I was obliged to present a pleasant face as our landlady knocked upon our door before leading in a young woman who I judged to be no more than twenty-five years old.

I am certain that my friend would already have deduced much more about her, but my own observations revealed that she was of medium height with hair of a rich dark brown shade, and that she was far from unattractive.

"Miss Agnes Lorimer, to see Mr Holmes," announced Mrs Hudson before leaving.

We had both risen as she entered, and now Holmes approached her.

"Miss Lorimer, welcome. I see that you are a little chilled, so pray come nearer the fire. I think you will find the basket chair to be comfortable."

"Thank you, sir," she replied. "I hope I have done right to consult you. It would grieve me to have wasted your time."

"I am sure that will not be the case," my friend smiled. "Shall I call for tea?"

"Thank you, sir, but no. I have to return to my work at the earliest moment."

"I am aware that a seamstress is expected to produce a daily quota, if she expects to retain her employment."

"How on Earth....."

"It is simplicity itself. The indentations on your fingers from the constant pushing of needles into resistant fabrics are quite unmistakable."

She gave him an astonished look. "You amaze me, sir."

"To notice such things is a necessity of my profession. Now, I take it that the box you carry is in some way connected to your reason for visiting us today?" He paused, suddenly remembering my presence. "Forgive me, I should have introduced my friend and colleague Doctor John Watson, whose help has proven invaluable in many of my enquiries. I assure you that he is the soul of discretion."

I moved towards her and we shook hands.

When we were seated, she elaborated. "This box arrived with the morning post at my home in Hampstead. As you see, it is sealed. I have made no attempt to open it because of this accompanying note." She passed an envelope to Holmes, who immediately held it up to catch the light.

"Rather cheap quality paper," he observed as he withdrew the enclosed sheet, "with no watermark. But let us see what this tells us."

He gave the paper a momentary glance, before holding it up so that I could read it:

Miss Lorimer,

Do not open the box.

See Sherlock Holmes.

"So you see why I have brought it to you," she said then.

She held the box out to Holmes, who took it and shook it slightly while holding it near his ear.

"It weighs much less than I would have expected, in fact it is very light." He paused before asking her, "Is there no one known to you who could have sent this?"

"No one, sir. I spend most of my time with my mother who lives with me, or at my place of employment. I have few friends or acquaintances."

"So it is unlikely that this could be a practical joke?"

"I cannot imagine who would play such a trick."

"Is there, forgive me for asking this, a suitor, perhaps?"

"I have had but one, sir, but we quarrelled and he went to sea. I have not heard from him since, nor do I wish to."

Holmes regarded her thoughtfully. "Tell us, pray, how long ago was this?"

"Almost three years, now."

He nodded, rose and went to his desk, where he picked up the straight-bladed knife that he often used to open letters. He ran the sharp edge around the box, beneath the lid.

"As I thought. It was secured by nothing more than common wood glue."

Nevertheless he raised the lid slightly with caution, peering into the box through the narrow space that was created. After a moment of inspection he folded it back to its fullest extent, visibly becoming more relaxed and with the ghost of a smile playing on his lips.

"Why," I said with some bewilderment, "it appears to be empty."

"Not quite," Holmes corrected, taking from it a piece of white card.

Miss Lorimer and I leaned forward, to see that the card bore nothing but a symbol. It was a serpent's head, but unlike any serpent that I have ever seen. It had horns, and fangs much longer than what is normal, and its eyes glittered unmistakably with vengeful hate.

My friend stared at the card, then turned it over in his hand. His face was expressionless as he held it up so that our visitor and I could obtain a better view.

"Does this device have any significance for you Miss Lorimer?"

She shivered visibly. "None. It is a horrible thing."

"It is a mythological or imaginary creature I am sure, but you are quite certain that this is the first that you have seen of it?"

"I am, but why would anyone send such a thing to me?"

"In order to bring you here, as I will demonstrate in a moment. The real question is, I think, why was this meeting desired and arranged."

Holmes placed the card on a side-table, and took up a volume of his index.

"This is where I retain details and objects connected with enquiries from prospective clients which fail to develop. When I saw the card, I knew at once that the device was familiar."

He withdrew a similar card and replaced the file. I saw that the embossed hideous head was now underlined with an address. Both Miss Lorimer and I craned our necks to read it:

J. Farrar,

Solicitor,

42, Clapham High Street.

"When did this arrive?" I asked him.

"A few months ago. When I received no explanation I put it aside, in case clarification was to follow. None did, until now."

"So are we to visit Mister Farrar, this morning?"

"That would seem to be an obvious first step of our enquiry." He turned to our visitor. "Miss Lorimer, We will see what can be learned from this, today. I see that you are anxious to return to your work. If you will be so good as to leave your address with Doctor Watson, I think I can promise that you will hear from us very soon. No," he anticipated her next question, "you need not be concerned about fees. On this occasion there will be none."

He brushed aside her effusive thanks and gestured for me to accompany her outside, where I was able to procure a hansom quickly. She appeared much relieved as she left me.

#

Mr Jonathan Farrar was huge. As Holmes and I seated ourselves in front of his desk I saw that he literally overflowed from his chair. The buttons of his waistcoat strained against his bulk, and the excess flesh of his cheeks quivered as he spoke.

"No, sirs," he rumbled in answer to Holmes' enquiry, "this rather frightening illustration is not my doing. I was instructed to add my details to the card and send it to your goodself by a client. It was some little time ago, as I remember."

"You were given no explanation?"

"None. When I attempted to extract one, the client said that you would understand – eventually."

"Do you recall the name of this man?" I asked, anticipating Holmes' next question.

Mister Farrar nodded. "Oh I do, sir, I do. It was Mr Alwyn Doubleday. I fear you will learn nothing from him though for, as you have doubtless read in the newspapers, he died recently in Newgate."

"Consumption, I believe."

"Breathing was a great effort for him, as I recall."

"Is there anything more you can tell us, to assist our enquiry?" Holmes asked.

Mr Farrar shook his head, his jowls quivering as he fingered his moustache, then his expression brightened. "Of course, it almost slipped my memory, sirs. The very reason that Mr Doubleday consulted me was to instruct me to retain an envelope until you came here, as you have today."

With that he rose from his chair, the effort reddening his face. He waddled across the room to a picture of Her Majesty upon the panelled wall and slid it aside to reveal a small safe. The envelope that he withdrew he handed to Holmes, who gave it a momentary glance before placing it in his pocket.

Mr Farrar closed the safe and smiled at us expectantly, and I formed the impression that he had become curious about the contents of the envelope after having retained it for some time. Holmes had no intention of opening it in his presence however, for he rose immediately and I did likewise.

"My thanks to you, Mr Farrar. Doubtlessly this will be of considerable aid to our investigation. Good morning to you, sir."

We left the solicitor's premises then, leaving him with an expression of sad disappointment. My friend said nothing more until we had walked a short distance along Clapham High Street. I made to raise my stick as an empty hansom passed, but he placed a restraining hand on my arm.

"One moment, Watson. The contents of this envelope may determine our next destination."

He tore at the flap with a thumbnail, after remarking on the lack of weight of the envelope.

"Perhaps it is empty." I suggested. "But then, what purpose could there be in all this?"

We stood aside to allow a woman accompanied by five children to pass, as he withdrew a single playing card.

"So," he said, "what have we here?"

He held it up so that I could examine it. It was a ten of hearts, but the figure had been added to by a scratchy pen, so that it bore the legend: '+1'.

"What can it mean, Holmes?" I asked.

He smiled. "It seems we have eleven hearts to consider then. Does that suggest anything to you?"

I shook my head, but in a moment it came to me. "Of course. There is an inn of that name in Chelsea that I noticed when we were there recently. It was once called 'The Plough and Sickle' but has been renamed after restoration from fire damage."

"Excellent, Watson. Now we can proceed, if you will be good enough to summon that cab which has just turned the corner."

He was silent during most of the journey, which is often his custom. I also made no comment, except to exclaim as an elderly beggar crossed the road without raising his head, the horses' hooves narrowly missing his thin body.

We alighted and the cab left us. I saw that the inn nestled between a saddlery and the premises of a maker of walking-canes. Holmes looked up at the sign above us that swung slightly in the breeze.

"Not quite as we envisaged, old fellow."

I saw his meaning. The sign bore the image of eleven harts, animals as distinct from the depictions of the human heart that we had imagined. Nevertheless, he appeared to be satisfied that this was the place we sought.

We entered through a door that was propped open. The air was heavy with smoke and several tables were occupied by men talking quietly. Behind the bar a man who could have been an ex-boxer stood polishing glasses with a dirty towel. Holmes wished him good day and he nodded silently.

"What can I get you gentlemen?" he asked then.

A man in a crumpled suit who had been leaning against the bar nearby pushed himself upright and staggered past us, sodden with drink. My friend waited until the fumes had dispersed, before answering.

"First tell me, landlord, have you been here for some time, or have you taken up your post since the recent fire."

The man raised his eyebrows in surprise. "Well sir, I have owned this place since long before that. Why do you ask?"

"I wondered if this is familiar to you." He produced the card that our client had brought.

"I have seen it before," he said with a puzzled expression. Then his brow cleared. "Of course. Just wait a minute, sir. I remember now."

With that he vanished through the beaded curtain that presumably concealed his living quarters. He reappeared after a few minutes, bearing a flat cardboard case with a wax seal. I saw that the serpent's head symbol was embossed on both sides.

Holmes made to reach for it but the barman held it back.

"No, sir. My instructions were to open it in your presence, should you call, and read to you the contents." He broke the seal and folded back the flap.

"Why," he said after extracting a small sheet of cheap paper, "it is just an address. It says: 19, Paradise Street, Hammersmith."

"Can you recall the person who left this with you?"

The barman adopted a thoughtful look, excused himself and left us for a moment to serve a customer. He quickly returned looking pleased with himself.

"I can't rightly remember when it was, sir, but the man who paid me to keep this for you was about as tall as your friend here. I thought at the time that he had been in a fight. I used to be in that game myself so I know what a man who's had a good battering looks like. His lip was swollen or scarred. I can't think of anything else, except that his voice was queer."

"Do you mean that it was deep," I asked, "or hoarse?"

He shook his head. "Not deep sir, the very opposite. It was more like a squeak, and I can't say that I'd ever heard another like it."

"Can you recall anything more?" Holmes enquired.

The innkeeper reflected. "I can't say that I can, sir. He wore a long coat, I think, and his hat was pulled down over his face so that I could hardly see his eyes, but that's about all."

"My thanks to you, landlord."

"Can I pull you gentlemen a drink, sir?" He placed a hand on the handle in anticipation.

Holmes glanced at the dirty towel. "Not now, thank you. We are involved in matters that require us to keep a clear head." He produced a half-sovereign from his pocket. "But pray take this for your most valuable help."

The landlord accepted this with thanks and we left.

We emerged as a hansom delivered its passenger to a house across the street. Before it could take off, we were there in a few quick strides. Holmes gave our destination as Baker Street, and the horse broke into a fast trot.

"I have observed the signs of impending hunger in your expression, Watson," he explained, "so I thought it best that we should consume the late lunch which Mrs Hudson is undoubtedly keeping for us, before visiting Hammersmith."

The roast duck was indeed welcome, although Holmes ate little of it. No sooner had I finished my gooseberry pie and coffee, than he rose quickly from his chair to put on his coat and hand me mine. In moments, we were strolling along Baker Street awaiting the appearance of a cab. Our wait was a short one.

"Well, Watson," Holmes said as we set off, "we will now see where the next clue in this rather ridiculous paper-chase leads us."

Paradise Street cannot have been named by anyone who was familiar with the place. It was no more than a short block of adjoined dwellings, both sides of the street being similar, situated at the very extremity of Hammersmith where the countryside resumed. The pavement was uneven and muddy, so that we had to tread carefully.

"The house second from the end is number 19, Holmes" I remarked as we progressed.

He nodded. "And the occupier is already aware of our impending visit. The curtains moved as he observed our approach."

We stepped over the puddles along the short path, and he rapped upon the door with his stick. The owner, a young fellow barely into his twenties, I judged, must indeed have been expecting us, for he emerged immediately.

"What are you gentlemen wanting here?"

My friend ignored his coarse manner. "Good afternoon. We are conducting a legal investigation." He held up Mr Farrar's card for the man to see. "Kindly tell us, does this symbol have any significance for you? There seems to be some connection with this district."

The man peered at the card with a blank expression, and shook his head. I knew instantly, as Holmes certainly did, that we were confronting the individual described by the landlord of The Eleven Harts, whose hare lip (not the result of blows, as the landlord had surmised) was very noticeable.

"I know nothing of this," he replied in a high-pitched voice that was further proof of his identity. His eyes took on a shifty look as he added, "You must have the wrong place."

"So it would appear," my friend retorted. "Yet our informant was quite certain. You are quite sure, Mr....."

"Edward Knell. I told you that I know nothing." He scowled at us and sarcastically wished us good day, before closing the door firmly.

"Surly fellow," I remarked as we retraced our streps. "He is the one the innkeeper spoke of, undoubtedly."

"His appearance confirms it, as does his response when he set eyes upon the serpent's head. I feel sure that we will see more of him before long, but for now we will walk into Hammersmith in search of a hansom."

#

Holmes poured two glasses of port from the crystal decanter. We had returned to Baker Street without incident, and dinner was still an hour away.

"As far as I can tell," he said when we had settled into our armchairs and taken our first sips, "presenting this symbol has acted as a kind of signal for a sequence of events to begin. Miss Lorimer was directed to involve us, then we in turn were sent to Mr Farrar who supplied us indirectly with the name of the inn. From there we visited Mr Edward Knell. I confess that I cannot yet see the reason behind this."

"Perhaps," I answered after taking a further drink, someone with a strange sense of humour wishes to waste our time."

"Possible but unlikely, I think. Ah, of course, I should have remembered earlier." Holmes reached for his index and turned its pages rapidly. After a moment he stopped to read, nodding his head silently. When he replaced the volume he had the look of someone enlightened.

"What have you learned, old fellow?" I enquired.

"You will recall that Mr Farrar mentioned a client who died in Newgate."

"I believe he named him as Alwyn Doubleday."

"Precisely, although that was but one of the identities adopted by this adept professional jewel thief. I knew I had heard of him before, but the details escaped me. His method, it seems, was always the same. The victims were invariably widows or elderly women, always with a sizeable collection of valuable jewellery. He was known to have been disturbed on several occasions during nighttime burglaries, and to have viciously attacked the helpless owners of the gems he was in the process of stealing. It was his last escapade that landed him in prison, for the lady screamed loud enough to attract the attention of a passing constable. Doubleday was arrested, but she almost died."

"Hardly a gentleman," I commented. "It sounds as if Newgate was no more than he deserved."

"Quite," Holmes agreed. "He was of course given a long sentence, and was reported to have become insane as a result of his incarceration. Perhaps that was when he devised this little puzzle."

I was about to reply, but was interrupted by the chimes of the door-bell. Mrs Hudson's answering voice preceded a heavy tread upon the stairs.

"It is Lestrade," My friend said with certainty.

We rose expectantly, as the inspector entered after knocking.

"Come in, Lestrade," Holmes said in his most welcoming tone. "Place your hat on that side-table, then be seated and help yourself to a cigar."

The inspector complied except for the cigar, which he declined.

"No thank you, Mr Holmes. I have not much time. I am here because we received information from an anonymous informant that a young woman, a Miss Agnes Lorimer, is in possession of the stolen tiara belonging to the Countess Woolby. We called at Miss Lorimer's address and, after calming her hysterical mother, searched her room. It did not take us long to discover that the information was correct. I arrested her of course, but she claims innocence and to be your client."

"And so she is," Holmes shifted his slim form in his chair. "But more importantly, did Miss Lorimer's mother mention any visitors of the last few hours?"

The official detective looked confused. "Yes, as a matter of fact she referred to a gas fitter who called earlier to attend to a suspected leak in her daughter's room. When we arrived, she at first thought it was him returning."

"Did the lady draw your attention to anything unusual about him?"

"I think...." Lestrade consulted his notebook. "Yes, here it is. She said he had a squeaky voice, like a character from a Punch and Judy show."

Surprisingly, Holmes laughed. "Inspector, I suggest that you ask Miss Lorimer if she knows of this man. If she denies it you may release her, for the visitor was an associate of a deceased criminal who is the subject of my current investigation. The object was to implicate her, for reasons I expect to discover shortly, in his past crimes. I am sure that the Countess will be grateful for the return of her property."

Lestrade nodded after some little consideration, and left soon after. Holmes smiled as he lit his clay pipe.

"Miss Lorimer will soon be back at her home," he said, as he sat wreathed in fragrant smoke. "I think Mr Edward Knell must have acted immediately after we left him. This affair appears increasingly as a predetermined sequence of events, begun by the appearance of that serpent's head symbol. Alwyn Doubleday, in his madness, must have planned them carefully."

"If that is the case, I wonder how the sequence will develop."

"Doubtlessly this will be revealed to us soon, possibly tomorrow."

Holmes said little during dinner. I saw that he was preoccupied, and had no doubt that it was on some feature of the case that Miss Lorimer had brought to us.

"What perplexes me," he murmured, more to himself than as an opening to a conversation, "is the link between our client and myself. Why was the box sent to her, and why was she instructed to bring it to me?"

This did not occupy his thoughts for long, however. When our meal was concluded we adjourned to our armchairs as was our custom, to spend the remaining hours before retiring in the promised discussion of his foreign adventures. Holmes was in that rare mood where he would elaborate on his past exploits, so I took notes as we smoked cigars and partook of some excellent brandy.

The evening passed surprisingly quickly. Before we were aware of it, midnight approached and we parted.

#

Holmes had already finished his breakfast before I joined him the following morning.

"I see that you have enjoyed a very large kipper," I remarked after greetings had been exchanged.

He nodded. "You deduced that from the size of the bones that remain on my plate. Excellent, Watson. Allow me to summon Mrs Hudson so that you may consume a similar meal."

This he did and we spoke sparingly as I ate until our landlady appeared to ask if we required more coffee and to bring the early editions of several newspapers. We declined the additional beverage and she cleared the table with her usual efficiency. I was about to adjourn to my armchair and to enquire of Holmes his intentions for the day, when his expression suddenly became grim.

"This affair becomes more curious still." He handed me the folded newspaper. "Look at this, Watson."

He retrieved his old briar and began to fill it as I gazed at the headline he had indicated:

CLAPHAM SOLICITOR FOUND STRANGLED.

I did not need to read the accompanying article to know that it was Mr Farrar who had met a sudden and violent end. More curious still, as my friend had said.

"What can this mean?" I asked him.

He put his pipe aside. "Clearly Mr Farrar was part of this pattern that is proving so elusive to define. Very well, we have one certain connection to this affair, and this morning we will make use of it."

"Are you referring to Mr Edward Knell?"

"I am. We know that, despite his denial, he is involved in this affair, since he visited Miss Lorimer's house soon after we questioned him. Let us see what he will tell us when confronted with his actions." He rose and approached the hat-stand. "Here, Watson, put on your hat and coat and we will attempt to procure the hansom that I have just seen from the window before it is taken."

We were back at the outskirts of Hammersmith before mid-morning. Our driver had controlled his horse with difficulty, as the animal was skittish and, I would have said, without much experience of hauling cabs through the streets of the capital.

This time we saw no indication that Mr Knell had observed our approach. Again Holmes rapped urgently on the door with his stick, but it was more than a few moments before it was flung open to reveal the occupant half-dressed and with traces of shaving-soap behind his ears.

His face changed from expectation to fury as he recognised us.

"I told you yesterday that you are wasting your time," he said in his shrill voice. "If you don't leave instantly, I'll have the law on you."

"That, I think, would be more to your inconvenience than ours," my friend answered.

"What do you mean by that?" Mr Knell's face reddened, as he scrutinized Holmes. "And who are you anyway?"

"My name is Sherlock Holmes."

His manner changed instantly. Fear showed in his eyes.

"You said you were from the legal people, before."

"I said that Doctor Watson and myself are conducting a legal investigation, which is true. I see from your expression that you have heard of me, so you are possibly aware that you will fare better by being straight with us now than you would at Scotland Yard."

"Why should I. I ain't done nothing wrong."

Holmes gave him a look of mock-disappointment. "You believe then, that entering the house of my client, Miss Agnes Lorimer, in order to leave false evidence against her before informing the official force, was a lawful act? Come now, Mr Knell. Many of your recent activities are known to us, but a full account is necessary if I am to conclude this case successfully. For my part, I will guarantee in return to give no aid to Scotland Yard in their investigation into the affairs of the late Alwyn Doubleday."

At this last it must have come home to the young Mr Knell that we were in possession of much that could be used against him. At Holmes' words his expression changed, then collapsed into a countenance of despair as he put his hands to his face and sat down heavily on his doorstep.

"Alwyn Doubleday was my uncle," he told us in his squeaky tones. He took a moment to collect himself and I saw that he fought to restrain tears. "More of a father to me than my own, he was. He was a thief, I know that, and that he had a temper that was easily roused, but murder he would not have done, and neither would I." He looked up at us like a hunted beast, with the scar on his lip swollen and vivid.

"Who then, since you are aware of the crime and deny your guilt, is the murderer of the solicitor, Mr Jonathan Farrar?"

"The same as who threatened and blackmailed my uncle, and is the blight of my life."

"You must tell us his name," I specified.

He spoke slowly, not meeting our eyes. "It is Roger Burcott, and a worse scoundrel you will never meet."

"Rarely, at least." Holmes agreed. "I had thought him dead, or retired from his wicked pursuits."

"You know of this man?" I asked my friend.

"By reputation only, for our paths have never crossed. He was suspected, some years ago, of the kidnapping of a six year-old child who was subsequently found dead despite a ransom being paid, but the charge was never proved. He has a history of extortion and the heinous crime of 'adopting' children from the orphanages of our city, only to sell them to foreign clients to work as slaves in the fields of distant lands."

"The man is a blackguard!" I exclaimed. "An absolute disgrace."

"Quite so, but let us hear what Mr Knell has experienced."

"Years ago," the young man began, "my uncle was discovered burgling a house in the early hours on a small estate in Kent. He was about to leave with his booty when he was attacked by an elderly butler. My uncle did not hurt the man, I swear, but shook off his restraining hold in order to make his escape. The butler fell and struck his head, which killed him as his master entered the room and held my uncle at gunpoint. My uncle was certain that this would mean the law and a long sentence or the rope, but was amazed when Roger Burcott, for it was he, told him that he was free to go. Burcott explained that the body would be disposed of in such a way that my uncle would be seen to be responsible, and in addition several witnesses could be paid to testify to his guilt. All this could be avoided as long as he remembered that he now worked for Burcott, who was to be his master until the day he died."

I found this appalling, but Holmes seemed to experience no surprise.

"This is despicable, but no less than I would expect if the man's reputation does him justice. Tell us then, the significance of Roger Burcott's involvement in this affair."

Mr Knell appeared to struggle with his recollections, before continuing. "When he learned of my closeness to my uncle, he drew me into his web, as I began to see it. His further threat was that I would meet with a sudden 'accident' if either of us failed to obey his every word. My uncle's skills as a burglar continued to be controlled by Burcott, as did my life. Under his direction I have committed crimes of which I will always be ashamed."

Holmes nodded. "But how does our client, Miss Agnes Lorimer feature in these events?"

"Do you gentlemen recall the murderess Kathleen Dinwell?"

"It would be extraordinary if we did not. The dailies were full of her crimes and subsequent execution, less than a year ago."

"She was engaged to be married to Burcott, but that did not prevent him from sending her to do his dirty work when he felt she could be useful. There was a debt to be collected from a party in Whitechapel, a man whose luck had deserted him at a card game. In some way, I don't know how, the money became due to Burcott and he sent Miss Dinwell to collect. She also was a hard and dishonest woman, but the debtor believed he could be rid of her by force. He knocked her to the ground and told her to inform her master that he wouldn't pay and that was the end of it, and she replied by burying a kitchen knife in his chest. By the time the constables arrived she had fled, and was arrested in Hampstead later that day. Before she was captured she attempted to find a hiding-place by forcing her way into the house of a young woman who had looked out in response to the commotion and sounds of police whistles."

"Miss Agnes Lorimer," I ventured.

"It was. That lady slammed the door and the fugitive was captured. Burcott swore revenge on her, for he attributed her refusal of assistance to the loss of his mate. All this my uncle knew because Burcott planned to use him to ensure that the girl met a painful death, but he had no stomach for it. Secretly he devised a plan in which I was to be instrumental. You would be drawn in to protect her, then in stages the situation would be revealed to you through the solicitor and others. It was intended to end with you receiving enough evidence to send Roger Burcott to the gallows, but before that could be arranged my uncle was apprehended by the official force and himself imprisoned. Before long he was afflicted by consumption and then insanity, and his plan was left incomplete. During his last days I visited him in his cell so that I might further his intentions, but he hardly knew me. By this time Burcott had discovered my uncle's treachery, as he saw it, and concocted an alternative scheme. When he demanded that I implicate Miss Lorimer in the theft of the tiara it was because he had already arranged that she should be murdered in prison, and Mr Farrar was disposed of because of his part in my uncle's plan."

"By whom?" I interrupted.

"In truth I know not, but Burcott was so enraged that it is likely that he could well have acted personally."

"And the serpent's head symbol?" Holmes enquired.

"That was a simple device to ensure that the events were understood to be a succession. Such a hideous depiction is not easily forgotten by most. My uncle was determined that every stage of his plan should be connected in the correct manner, as it would have been if things had turned out as he intended."

"Why did you not confess this to us yesterday?" Holmes fixed him with a stern glare. "Mr Farrar's life may have been saved."

Mr Knell shook his head. "You do not understand, sir. If Roger Burcott orders that you shall die then you will, before long. That is why I would not talk to you yesterday, because of my fear of him. He has already threatened my life and will doubtlessly end it when our conversation becomes known to him, as it surely will. One of his boasts is that he has ears everywhere, but I have relented and spoken out for my uncle's sake."

His narrative ended, the young man sat with his head bowed.

Holmes was silent for what seemed a long time, and I did not intrude upon his thoughts.

"So, Mr Knell," he said at last. "I can see nothing to indicate that you have not been truthful. Your criminal acts cannot be condoned, but I will keep my word to you and Scotland Yard shall hear nothing of this from me. You can be assured that Roger Burcott's days are numbered, for he cannot be allowed to continue even if the law has no grounds to prevent him. As for you, I accept that you are in mortal danger since Burcott's accomplices may strike before I am able to deal with him." He reached into his coat and produced several banknotes. "My advice to you is to lock up your property and leave without delay. If you spend several weeks abroad it may well be sufficient for me to remove the threat that hangs over you, but we will see. Here is enough to sustain you for that amount of time plus a little more. I suggest you repair to the docks without delay. Come, Watson."

With that we turned away abruptly to leave the dejected fellow stammering his surprised thanks. We had made our way to the nearby road in search of a cab, before I spoke.

"You never cease to surprise me, Holmes."

He shrugged. "His crimes were mostly forced upon him. I do not think that he will continue them when he returns. But now we have a new adversary to deal with, and I must give some thought to what must be done. This Burcott must be a man of some ability, both because he is the head of an organised criminal gang with some influence and because he keeps himself concealed to the extent that I have not heard of his activities lately. So, old fellow, after we have fortified ourselves with Mrs Hudson's chicken pie, I think a visit to our friend Inspector Lestrade is indicated."

#

Mid-afternoon had arrived by the time we found ourselves seated in Lestrade's office. We had already refused his offer of tea, which we knew from past experience to be an appalling concoction.

"Well, gentlemen," he said from across his battered desk, "I had not expected to see you again so soon. What brings you here today?"

"Firstly," Holmes answered, "I would like to know the outcome of your dealings with Miss Lorimer."

"She was released. Acting on your recommendation, I accepted her denials. Unfortunately, we have not yet apprehended whoever placed the stolen tiara in her room. The Countess Woolby, by the way, was delighted at its return."

"Doubtlessly you will discover some connection between that theft and the subject of my current enquiry."

"Ah yes," Lestrade remembered, "you mentioned that you were investigating the misdeeds of someone deceased. Really, Mr

Holmes, here at the Yard we have enough to do looking into the crimes of the living."

"That is all over. The man I would like to discuss is Roger Burcott."

The conversation paused as there occurred a burst of activity in the corridor outside. Heavy footfalls and shouted protests faded into echoes before the official detective continued:

"Now there is a man I would dearly like to see behind bars. Without consulting his file, I can tell you that he is guilty of kidnapping, the robbery last year of two solid silver statuettes from storage as they awaited exhibition in the British Museum and, quite possibly, murder. The worst of it is that we can prove nothing against him. Every charge has been dropped because he has produced witnesses who claim he was in their company when the crime occurred."

"Drawn from members of his gang, no doubt." I speculated.

"Naturally, Doctor. Are you investigating any incident in particular?"

"We believe him to be implicated in the murder of a solicitor, Mr Jonathan Farrar," Holmes said.

The inspector's surprise was evident. "But that was only yesterday! You are quick off the mark with this one, gentlemen. Gregson took several constables to Clapham but learned little, so I understand."

He failed to keep the satisfaction out of his voice, and I reflected that the old rivalry persisted.

"So nothing has been discovered to indicate who is responsible?"

"Not yet, but we will get him, Mr Holmes, you can be assured."

"But in the interval, are you able to disclose to us the whereabouts of Roger Burcott?"

"As always, we have no reason to suspect a connection, but seeing as it's you, I can tell you that he lives at 21, Galatia Gardens, Knightsbridge."

"My thanks to you, Inspector." Holmes got to his feet as did I.

Lestrade called after us as we retreated. "You will inform me of any significant developments?"

"As ever. Good afternoon."

We emerged from that drab building looking for a hansom.

"Are we bound for Clapham, or Galatia Gardens," I asked my friend.

"Mr Farrar's Clapham office is unlikely to tell us much, Watson, since Gregson and several heavy-booted constables have trodden all over any evidence that might have remained. Galatia Gardens we will leave until tomorrow, I think. So, for now, I believe that a brandy in anticipation of a hearty meal will be in order."

Our dinner was indeed excellent. Surprisingly, Holmes ate unusually well, though he appeared weary. After only an hour or two of smoking and conversation, during which we discussed once more the disturbing rise of German influence in Europe, he announced his intention to retire. As the door of his room closed behind him I began the final chapters of a rousing sea saga that I had been attempting to read for some weeks, but fell asleep before I reached its conclusion.

My friend maintained a thoughtful silence during breakfast. I made only the occasional remark, since it became apparent that he was making plans towards our progress in this affair. Finally, with our landlady having removed the remains of our meal, he took up his violin. For almost an hour I endured the mournful tones of what must surely have been one of his own compositions, all the while attempting to reduce my accumulated pile of medical journals.

When the appalling noise ceased suddenly, I knew that his mood had lifted.

"Ho, friend Watson," he said cheerfully. "Time to leave, I think. There is heavy rain to contend with, so let us not forget our umbrellas."

Unusually, our driver seemed uncertain as to our destination. It was received with a puzzled look and we eventually arrived after fruitless visits to addresses adjoining Hyde Park and Sloane Street, before Beauchamp Place proved to lead to the place we sought. As we alighted it was immediately apparent why our youthful driver had experienced such confusion. Galatia Gardens was all but hidden from the road, the only access being through a narrow corridor between two stately mansions. Anyone visiting here would have stated the main thoroughfare as their destination, then walked beneath the sprawling oak and along the passage to reach the crumbling structures beyond.

Gripping our umbrellas against the incessant weather, we emerged into a three-sided square. The remaining side featured a path leading to communal gardens which were now bereft of vegetation but must once have been more extensive, since classical statues bearing evident signs of neglect stood atop a slope in the near distance. Number 21 appeared to be the sole inhabited dwelling, the other four appearing equal in age but now obviously derelict.

"A dull place," I commented.

"Possibly not without purpose," Holmes observed. "Someone with much to conceal as Burcott undoubtedly has, would do well to purchase adjacent buildings to his chosen lair, especially in such an out-of-the-way location. His activities would not fare well with public exhibition."

The house at first appeared deserted, but after we had ventured a few yards along the path the door flew open. A rough-looking fellow in worn tweeds called to us angrily:

"What are you doing here? This property is private!"

He strode up to us aggressively, but Holmes replied in a calm voice.

"Our apologies, sir. We are strangers here who have been given directions to Hyde Park, apparently incorrectly."

"Well, the way isn't here, is it? Be off with you before I make you sorry."

"Very well. Tell me, is this the only exit?"

The man scowled. "You can't see that, can't you? Get out of here!"

We retraced our steps, saying nothing until we reached Beauchamp Place.

"Offensive brute," I remarked then. "A lesson in manners would not go amiss."

Holmes smiled. "I do so agree, Watson, but he has inadvertently provided us with a possible way to conclude this case. I had considered six separate more elaborate paths for us to follow, but hopefully these will now be unnecessary."

"I cannot see that we have learned anything."

"On our return to our lodgings, I may be able to enlighten you after consulting my index."

I shook my head as we regained the main road. "I confess to being all at sea, regarding this."

Holmes adjusted the angle at which he held his umbrella. "My first thought, on entering that square, was to obtain an overall view of the house with the intention of paying Mr Burcott an overnight visit in search of evidence, hence our venturing a short distance along that path." He signalled and a passing hansom came to a halt a short way ahead. "The appearance of that ruffian curtailed that however, but replaced my plan with a better one."

"Holmes, you mystify me. Nothing else occurred."

"Ah, but it did. Had you looked beyond our offensive friend, you would have seen several more of, presumably, Burcott's henchmen lurking in the open doorway at the ready. One of these I recognised as 'Fingers' Wood, a safecracker of some renown. He is our solution, and the way by which Burcott will finally be punished."

#

Holmes was still in the midst of his records as our landlady appeared bearing our luncheon. He waved away her warning that his food would quickly get cold if he did not partake of it soon, but joined me a few minutes later after finding the information he sought.

"I have information on Nathanial Wood's past, Watson. Not enough to secure a conviction, but perhaps he can be made to believe otherwise."

I pushed away my empty plate. "We are to visit him, then?"

"He is likely to stay in Galatia Gardens for some hours, since his most likely reason for being there is that Burcott has included him in some new crime he is planning which will require some hours of his time. He is called 'Fingers' because of his skill in opening safes and vaults, so most likely they intend an assault on a bank. I think we will allow him sufficient time to receive his instructions, before we interview him. He lives in Highgate, so how do you feel about an evening jaunt after dinner?"

"I am at your disposal."

"Good old Watson," he said before proceeding to eat. "And so we have the afternoon free. I see from *The Standard* that there is a recital at St James Hall. One of those little-known Lassus compositions, I believe."

"I would be delighted to accompany you."

#

The rain had long since ceased as we set out for Highgate. Clouds scudded across the sky, obscuring the moon at irregular intervals.

Holmes paid off the cab a short distance from our destination which, he explained, was a rather run-down street of terraced houses near the gasworks. We walked through several foul-smelling alleyways and two silent thoroughfares, before being confronted by a block of unlit dwellings with peeling paint and the occasional broken window repaired with newspaper.

"Mr Wood does not appear to have been a very successful criminal," I concluded." At least, he has spent little of his ill-gotten gains on accommodation."

"I know of at least six bank robberies, here and in the north of England, in which he was a definite participant," Holmes replied. "He has only served two jail sentences however, for minor crimes. Almost certainly he has a considerable sum hidden away, perhaps intended for his retirement."

We crossed the empty street to a house my friend indicated. A cat emerged from the shadows and preceded us, before disappearing up a passage which presumably led to the rear entrance. The place appeared to have once been a shop, for its window was large and square. Holmes peered through it from several angles before pronouncing the dwelling occupied.

"There is a glimmer of light in the room beyond the parlour. Let us see whether Mr Wood has returned."

He rapped upon the door with his stick, several times. After what seemed an age, I heard movement within.

Hinges, long starved of oil, creaked, and I caught a glimpse of the shadowy figure that was revealed. Holmes placed his foot where it would serve as an obstruction, as an attempt was made to slam the door hard.

"Good evening, Mr Wood," he said lightly. "After failing to meet you earlier, I thought we might make your acquaintance tonight."

Cautiously the occupier stepped out into the street, and I saw that he was a hulking brute of a man, heavy-set and hairless with small eyes that reflected the meagre glow from a nearby lamp-post.

"I don't know you," he said in a voice that was almost a growl. "What do you want?"

"I am surprised that you fail to recollect our visit to Galatia Gardens earlier since your current employer, Mr Roger Burcott, will undoubtedly have identified us. If he has not, you will certainly have heard of me. My name is Sherlock Holmes."

He shook his head. "That name means nothing to me." But his eyes belied his words.

"We are here to discuss your future."

At once, he became outraged. "What have my affairs to do with you?"

"Since I am aware of many of your past activities, the Newcastle Industrial Bank, for example, and the London & Provincial Mutual Society robberies, it might be to your advantage to listen to what I have to say."

"I wasn't there, when they were done."

"Ah, but you were. It hasn't been proven until now, but I can do so conclusively. Consider what that would mean in court, in addition to whatever you are involved in now." He glanced at me. "What would be your estimation, Watson?"

"Oh, best part of thirty years, I should think." I shrugged nonchalantly. "Unless anyone is or has been killed, of course. Then it's the rope."

In the poor light, I saw Mr Wood's expression change.

"If you want a cut of the loot, I might be able to arrange it," he said in subdued tones.

"My dear fellow," Holmes laughed. "That is not the case at all. You misunderstand our intention completely."

The safe-cracker appeared confused. "What do you want from me then, for you to keep quiet?"

Holmes let a few seconds pass. "It would be as well for you if you were to exclude yourself from Mr Burcott's current project, for our purpose is to ensure that he pays the penalty for his many crimes. Before you do this, it would be to your advantage and ours if you were to secretly procure evidence, some incriminating documents perhaps of his more serious misdeeds, and deliver them to us. An opportunity may well occur during your next visit to his house, or a subsequent occasion."

Mr Wood was visibly shocked. "I can't rat! Do you know what you're suggesting? I've heard about those who've tried this on him before, and none of them are alive now. I have never known of a more bitter and unforgiving man, and I've no wish to offend him."

"Yet if you continue on your present path you will certainly spend much of the rest of your life in prison, and I cannot imagine that you would relish that. Mr Burcott's intentions are known to Scotland Yard, as is your involvement, but if you follow my instructions nothing will be proved against you."

"Maybe the Yard couldn't touch me, but if I betray him then Burcott certainly would. If I don't do my part, he'll know something's up."

"Listen to Mr Holmes," I advised him. "He has said that we are here for the sake of your future. Follow his directions and you will stay a free man."

The safecracker turned his gaze on me momentarily, then looked at Holmes with narrowed eyes.

"You say the Yard knows about Burcott's job?"

Holmes nodded. "I have this from Inspector Lestrade himself."

"And if I get you something to put him away and don't take part in the job, I'll be left out of it?"

"I personally guarantee it."

"If I do this, how will I protect myself from him if he discovers what I've done before the job is done?"

"One moment," I interrupted. "How could it take place without you anyway? Is there another with your skill?"

"Burcott leaves little to chance. He's got Archie Berry, as a reserve."

"Another of your trade," Holmes confirmed. "But with a criminal history far worse than yours, I fancy. As to your question, my suggestion is that you take the *Glasgow Express* immediately after handing over the evidence to us. It departs from the capital every day and you will be conveyed to the station under my protection. When you arrive north of the border, you can decide upon your destination. Ireland, or if you wish to travel south after the misdirection, France may serve to conceal you until Burcott and his henchmen are convicted."

Mr Wood now appeared bewildered, as he wrestled with his dilemma. I feared that we had presented him with too much to consider.

"All right, Mr Holmes," he said at length. "I can see that I'll be better off doing as you say, provided that Burcott can't get his hands on me before he's captured. Where shall I bring the goods, if I can get them?"

"To Baker Street, or any other place you prefer."

"Baker Street will do."

"Are you certain that you will recognise the sort of information that is required?" Holmes asked.

For the first time, a faint smile crossed the safecracker's face. "I will know."

"Then we will expect to hear from you."

"As soon as I get something, you will have it."

"Then we will leave you. Good evening."

As we passed an unlit lamp-post I looked back once, but the street was again deserted.

#

"Do you believe we can trust the man?" I asked when we were settled back in our lodgings.

"Usually, I would have the gravest doubts," Holmes replied as he filled his clay pipe, "but the fear I saw in Mr Woods' face when I explained what awaited him after the certain failure of Burcott's plan reassures me. He may change his mind when he has considered further of course, but that is the risk we run."

As it was, a week passed and no word came. Holmes concerned himself briefly with the affair that I have described elsewhere as

222

'The Incident of the Broken Promise', but otherwise he spent much time adding to his index. The atmosphere in our rooms had, I felt, become one of anticipation. Daily, I saw his restlessness increase.

Then, late one stormy evening, a frantic rapping on our front door disturbed our peace. It ceased suddenly, to be instantly replaced by the repeated rings of the door-bell. I lowered the medical journal I had been reading, to see that Holmes was already on the landing and about to descend the stairs. The urgency was apparent but, not wishing to disturb Mrs Hudson at this hour, he had elected to answer the call himself. At once I put my reading aside, and rose with the intention of following. As I left our room I heard the front door close, and by leaning over the banister rail was able to see a bedraggled figure in oilskins preceding him in its ascent.

"Come in," my friend invited our visitor as they approached. "Watson, kindly be so good as to pour Mr Woods a brandy."

Our visitor removed his hat and I saw that he was indeed Mr Nathanial Woods. I handed him a full glass, as Holmes directed him to the basket chair.

"Thank you, sir," He said with an air quite unlike that he had displayed previously. "This really is most welcome."

He reduced the contents of the glass by about half in a single gulp.

When we were all three seated, Holmes leaned forward eagerly. "I see that you are quite upset, Mr Woods. Take some time to calm yourself while your drink has its restorative effect, and then tell us from the beginning what has transpired since our last meeting. I perceive that you had some difficulty in performing your task."

"You are right there, sir. There was me thinking I'd got away with it, when one of Burcott's closest accomplices walked in on me. I was shocked because of the care I'd taken, but something unexpected must have gone wrong. I gave him a good uppercut and left the place before the alarm was raised, but by now they'll be after me like a pack of hounds."

Holmes nodded. "As I have assured you, we will help you to leave the capital temporarily. Kindly be so good as to reveal what you were able to discover."

At this, Mr Woods plunged a hand into an inside pocket of his long oilskin coat. He retrieved a thick wad of papers. Some, I observed, were crumpled, while others seemed quite unused.

"I hope these are sufficient, Mr Holmes."

My friend accepted them and at once began to examine one page after another. Three or four minutes passed as Mr Woods and I waited in silence.

Finally, Holmes raised his head, and I saw triumph in his grey eyes.

"You have done well, Mr Woods. These are plans and outlines of crimes that have not yet taken place, as well as details of some which Scotland Yard are still investigating. Presumably Burcott retains these records for future reference, and that will prove to be his undoing. These documents will hang him, for they are in handwriting which is undoubtedly his own."

"Then I have done as you wanted?"

"Certainly. Now, unless there is anything else, it is time for us to arrange your departure."

Mr Woods drank again, and put down his empty glass on a side table. He got to his feet and ran a hand over his hairless head in a nervous gesture.

"Gentlemen, despite everything I am grateful for your help, but I am now a marked man, for certain."

Holmes said nothing but strode to the window and looked out from an oblique angle. After a few moments, he turned away and picked up his Bradshaw.

"Baker Street appears to be clear. I cannot see that we are under observation." He turned some pages quickly. "I had intended that you should leave London on the *Glasgow Express*, if you recall. I now see that it departed hours ago, but we are fortunate in that a slower train leaves Euston in a little over an hour." He replaced the book and turned to me. "Watson, our hats and coats, if you please. We will set off at once."

We left our lodgings quietly, to avoid disturbing our landlady. For some reason not disclosed to me, Holmes carried a small despatch-case. The rainfall was much reduced, but the strong wind remained. I had expected some difficulty in procuring a hansom at such a late hour, but to my surprise there were many in evidence. Holmes refused the first that presented itself, then the second, and we finally boarded a cab that discharged its passenger before us as we neared the end of Baker Street.

Little was said during the journey, but Mr Woods was visibly afraid. Every time a dark-clad figure appeared at the side of the road I could have sworn that he trembled, and every shadow in the ill-lit streets held terror for him. Holmes was vigilant in his many glances into the night, and I knew that any indication that all was not well would have produced a change in our destination, so I was relieved at our arrival.

The cab came to rest and we alighted, Holmes immediately inspecting this new scene as I paid our fare. We entered the station and purchased the ticket from a sleepy clerk, before ensuring that Mr Woods safely boarded the train that arrived after a short wait. The attending official raised a green flag and gave a blast on his whistle, before turning away as the last of the coaches disappeared into the darkness. Moments later all sounds of the conveyance ceased, and I saw that Holmes was studying the few travellers remaining on the platform. He turned his attention across the line, towards the waiting-room and benches at the opposite side of the track, and then left abruptly with me in his wake.

"Did you detect any observation?" I asked him as we left the station.

"No, there was no one. However, there is the possibility that Mr Woods was followed and observed entering our lodgings. The watcher could then have immediately left to report before I looked out on Baker Street. This may or may not be the case, but if so then Burcott is now aware of our interest in his affairs."

"My hand is on my service revolver at this moment."

"I also will be armed constantly, until this affair is over," he said as he selected a hansom from several nearby, awaiting the next exodus from the station.

I had anticipated that this affair, or the echoes of it, would be with us for some time. As it was, it came to a violent conclusion that very night. As our cab entered Baker Street, I saw Holmes become alert at once. His body stiffened as a hunting-dog's does, at the first sight of its prey.

"What is it?" I asked.

He shouted for the driver to halt. "Mr Woods seems to have been rather careless when he visited us. There are at least three roughs waiting for our return near our lodgings. I can only suppose that whoever followed Mr Woods reported to Burcott immediately, as I surmised earlier."

I peered into the darkness ahead. One of the lamp-posts held no illumination, whether because of malfunction or deliberate damage for the purpose of concealment by our adversaries I could not tell. I saw movement against the unlit buildings. The shadows would serve them well.

"I see them," I said, "and I am ready."

"You would serve me better by leaving, I think, Watson."

In the dim interior, I stared at him in surprise. "Holmes, whatever can you mean? As always, I am here to fight side-by-side with you."

"I do not doubt that for an instant, old fellow. But you must believe me when I tell you that to seek a constable or continue in this hansom to Scotland Yard would be by far the best course." He reached into his coat and extracted what I recognised to be the collection of papers provided by Mr Woods. "These must reach Scotland Yard tonight. I beg you to take them before we are accosted."

His intention was plain to see, that the evidence was delivered to Lestrade was clearly for the greater good. Yet I was reluctant in the extreme to leave my old friend to face an unknown number of opponents.

The decision was quickly taken from me, however. Holmes leapt from the cab and shouted to the driver: "Scotland Yard, with all speed."

The hansom lurched forward as the driver cracked his whip and the horse went into an immediate gallop. From the shadows a burly shape appeared and attempted to attach itself to the side of the conveyance, but I struck at the unshaven face through the open window and heard a scream as a wheel passed over the body. The driver shouted something that was lost on the wind as several shots pierced the silence. I looked back as best as I could but we were now too far away. Fear gripped me as I wondered whether my friend still lived, and the hansom leaned heavily to one side as we jolted around a sharp corner.

Then, and I thanked God for it, a young constable appeared out of the darkness. I shouted to the driver who brought the cab to a screeching halt, attracting the attention of the officer immediately. I leaped to the pavement, hurriedly explaining that the documents I placed in his hands were vital. He appeared confused, possibly he was new to the official force, but at the mention of Holmes' name and that of Lestrade he voiced his understanding and promised to send assistance as well as to effect delivery. I ushered him into the hansom before instructing the driver to resume his journey, and found myself alone in an instant. I began to retrace my steps, running in the ill-lit street from shadow to shadow and dreading what might lie ahead.

I slowed my pace to a cautious walk as I neared the scene. At once relief flooded over me because Holmes stood defiantly facing a tall man wearing a top hat, surrounded by four prone bodies and five vicious-looking roughs who appeared anxious to resume the assault.

I was by now breathless and still too far away to assist my friend, but as my heart slowed its beat I could hear what passed between them.

"You really must give it up, Mr Holmes. As soon as my agent brought me the news I realised the difficulties I would face in retrieving my property. No bullets remain in your weapon, you have only your swordstick with which to defend yourself. Be in no doubt that we will compel you to reveal to us where Nathaniel Woods is hidden and that it will be extremely painful, unless you choose to be sensible."

Moving silently, I drew nearer. In the meagre light I would swear that I saw Holmes' expression change to one of relief: his keen eyes had noticed my return. My service revolver was in my hand as I advanced further.

"Your criminal career is at end, Burcott. If I cannot, Scotland Yard will ensure it."

"You believe so?" He shifted his position, and the poor illumination revealed a thin, cruel face. His narrow moustache enclosed a mouth that snarled its evil intent. "Consider your situation, it does not support such an outcome." His voice took on a harsher edge, and he advanced towards my friend slowly. "Now return those papers, if you wish to die quickly."

In answer Holmes flung the despatch-case at his antagonist's feet obediently. As Burcott bent to retrieve it he screamed, and I saw that Holmes' swordstick protruded from his thigh. The others, armed with cudgels and knives, rushed forward, and the blade was withdrawn and buried in the chest of the first of them. The next man slashed at my friend and succeeded in drawing blood because Holmes' evasion came an instant too late, but no second attack was forthcoming. The assailant fell with my bullet in his heart, and another with blood gushing from his throat. The two remaining turned and saw me, and I was able to fell the nearest of them before he could get closer. The last man standing confronted me and I levelled my weapon at him but never fired, since he dropped his cudgel and fled into the night. I went to Holmes, who wiped blood from his face while holding his swordstick at the ready.

"Holmes," I cried. No!"

He glanced at me, unperturbed. "Oh, do not concern yourself, Watson. I have no intention of taking Burcott's life, only of ensuring that he does not attack further. You surely cannot imagine that I would cheat the hangman of so worthy a subject."

Before I could reply a police coach hurtled towards us out of the gloom, and then another. I counted eight armed constables emerging the instant their conveyances came to halt, accompanied by Inspector Lestrade.

He strode up to us, but stopped short to look at what surrounded him.

"I see that you and Doctor Watson have been busy, Mr Holmes. Constable Bramwell reported the urgency of the situation and I assembled these men before setting out at once." He turned his attention to Burcott, who was attempting to stem the flow of blood from his thigh. "But who have we here? I tell you, gentlemen, that if you have secured evidence against this man, you have done a good night's work indeed. The Yard has long hungered to see him behind bars, but our attempts until now have failed."

"You saw the papers that your constable delivered?" Holmes enquired.

Lestrade shook his head. "Not yet. He told me of their importance, so I placed them in our safe. It seemed to me that to furnish assistance was the most immediate issue."

"Quite so, Lestrade," he nodded. "And we thank you for it. The papers contain details of crimes past and present, written in Burcott's own hand. You should now have no difficulty in obtaining a conviction."

"We owe you a debt, sir," The official detective advanced upon us and saw my friend clearly for the first time. "But, Mr Holmes, you are wounded. Accompany us back to the Yard, where a police doctor will attend to you."

"My thanks," said Holmes, "but it is little more than a scratch. I think Burcott is in need more than I."

"I shall see to it. We want him to be in the best of health, when he mounts the scaffold." A burly sergeant had approached, and Lestrade turned to him. "Askins, leave two constables on guard here, while the rest of us return to the Yard. I will send out a conveyance to remove the bodies later."

The officer saluted and rejoined his men. Several windows nearby had been illuminated briefly, the residents disturbed by the reports from the firearms, but now all was dark once more.

"If there is nothing else, Inspector," said my friend, "Doctor Watson and myself will be away to our beds."

"Of course. I would appreciate a visit at the Yard tomorrow, to furnish a full report."

Holmes glanced at Burcott, whose stare exuded hate.

"It will our pleasure to do so."

We wished each other goodnight and the little detective set about organising their departure. Holmes and I walked wearily to our lodgings, and I saw that his bleeding has ceased.

"I confess to being glad to see the end of this day," I remarked.

Holmes placed his key in the lock. "I also, Watson. But, tired as we are, I am certain that you will have no objection to a brandy, before we surrender ourselves to a well-earned good night's sleep."